THE RUMOR

A Psychological Suspense Novella

Lori Lacefield

Cover designed by Lori Lacefield
Edited by Michelle Hope

This book is a work of fiction. Names, characters, places, and incidents either are products of the author's imagination or are used fictitiously. Any resemblance to actual persons, living or dead, events, or locales is entirely coincidental.

Lori Lacefield
Visit my website at www.LoriLacefield.com

Printed in the United States of America

First Printing: November 2018
Open Book Media, LLC

EBOOK ISBN-13 978-1-7322890-6-2
PAPERBACK ISBN – 13 978-1-7322890-7-9

CONTENTS

1

Haunted Halls

T wenty years. Beth had a hard time believing that much time had passed since she'd graced these tired halls. They still looked the same as she remembered: multi-speckled tile floors, walls made of concrete blocks painted white, fluorescent lights that flickered and emitted a constant hum. Handmade signs and posters hung from the walls at random: a plea for votes from a student council candidate, a reminder to order senior portraits by the deadline, an announcement for a dance after an early-November football game.

She skated her fingers along the wall, as if making a physical connection would help bring back old memories. She was happy the reunion committee had arranged for the guests to tour the old high school on the weekend, so they could reminisce free of current students and faculty. Other attendees had gone off to explore in pairs, but Beth wanted to be alone.

She glanced into the empty classroom where her favorite English teacher had once read a rousing edition of Edgar Allan Poe's "The Tell-Tale Heart". He'd doubled as a theater major in college and performed in the local Shakespearean festival every summer, so he was well versed in storytelling. She could still hear his thunderous voice, laced with an underlying menace, rise and lower as he spoke. She'd sat frozen in her chair as he'd paced the room, holding the book in his hand at chin level, and glancing over the top if it with a single eye, mimicking the veiled pale eye in the tale.

"Meantime the hellish tattoo of the heart increased. It grew quicker and quicker, and louder and louder every instant. The old man's terror must have been extreme! It grew louder, I say, louder every moment!—do you mark me well? I have already told you that I am nervous: so I am."

Those last words were but a whisper. Beth still got the chills thinking about them.

She stopped at the door of another room where she'd taken communications and headed up the yearbook committee. How much fun she'd had in that class, writing and editing articles, learning about layouts and photography. It had been the class that had later shaped her decision to work for a newspaper.

Gliding past the lockers, she chuckled at the recollection of the massive collage she and her best friend Joan had created inside their locker. Photographs of celebrity heartthrobs, snippets of words and phrases clipped from magazines, and their own drawings and art all stared out into the world every time they opened it. There were pictures of Joan and her posing and flashing the peace sign next to phrases like *Be Your Best Self* and *Go for It!* And hearts. So many hearts. Love, love, love.

Didn't we all just love each other back then?

She passed the bookstore where she worked two days a week during her time in Business Professionals of America to help develop her entrepreneurial skills, selling paper clips, notebooks, pencils, pens, erasers, power bars, energy drinks, and anything else students might need on the go. Headed up the stairs at the end of the hall, laughing all the way through the darkened E-wing, where couples came to sneak in quick make-out sessions after lunch and on breaks. She looked for the small etching of initials her then-boyfriend Nick had made near their favorite spot in a less visible corner. It was still there. *NS hearts BM.*

More hearts. In love. *Nicholas Storvik loves Beth McCallum.*

A small smile graced her lips.

It had been the first day of her freshman year, at the ripe age of fourteen, when Beth had decided that Nick Storvik—part-time lifeguard, quarterback of the mighty Vikings, and budding Nordic god—would be her future husband. It had only taken a single look, a flash of his pale blue eyes and bright smile as he shifted his attention ever so briefly away from his entourage to glance at her. Two weeks later they'd gone on their first date and never looked back. They were inseparable. Everybody always said so.

Except for one person. That other girl. She believed Nick belonged with *her.*

Beth immediately batted the thought of the girl away, like an annoying gnat.

The four years Beth and Nick had spent together in high school had mostly been happy. She knew how blessed they were—so many people she talked to about their high school experience groaned and ducked their head inside their hands like it was the most tortuous time on earth—but nearly everything Beth remembered about high school was positive. She'd never grown tired of learning, and except for biology where the teacher had forced her to dissect frogs and other various creatures, she'd enjoyed all her classes. Even those required classes she never would've chosen herself—like industrial arts, drafting, woodworking, and home economics—she'd loved them all.

She thought it was tragic how so many of the schools had now slashed those classes to save money. Some schools were even cutting choir and music and drama. And art. Art classes like the one where she'd created a miniature clay Viking mascot with her favorite player's number. Number seven. Nick's number, of course.

But Michigan, like the rest of the Midwest, had been hit hard by the recession in 2008, leaving school budgets in shambles and administrators scrambling to do more with less. Much less. It was no different in the small southwest Ohio community she and Nick lived in now.

The town they'd grown up in was a quaint lakefront community with a population of about eight thousand, just north of Ann Arbor, Michigan. It went without saying that the summer and autumn were the best times of the year there, summers spent swimming and water-skiing on the lake and attending the Fourth of July festivities highlighted by eating contests and the lighted parade of boats at night. Beth had always joined Nick's family on their boat, named *Susie Ann* after Nick's mother, as boats were not a luxury her parents could afford.

Football games dominated the autumn, as Beth spent Friday nights on the sidelines leading the cheers for Nick and her Saturdays sitting with his family in the "Big House"—as they referred to Michigan Stadium—clad in sweater and jeans, rooting for the Wolverines. She recalled how the smell of grilled burgers and brats constantly permeated the air from all the tailgate parties nearby. All of this was highlighted, of course, by the stunning fall foliage, always Beth's favorite, a carpet of orange, red, and yellow under a late-autumn sun that seemed to go on forever.

Idyllic, really, and yet, even with all those great memories and the addition of nights spent preparing for homecoming in a nearby warehouse decorating the floats, banners, and wagons that they used to parade the homecoming king and queen candidates around the stadium, there was always something about that time of year that left Beth with a deep-seated anxiety. Beneath all those times of such fun and innocence lay a disturbance she couldn't finger, one that clawed and scratched at her from the inside, like a trapped and desperate animal wanting to escape.

And she didn't like it. The way it wouldn't leave her alone.

Back in the lobby near the entrance to the school, she stopped before the trophy case and peered inside. The school had added several new accolades to the case since their graduation in 1998, but the big trophy from their year was still there—the state 3A football championship. And there, next to the trophy, a photo of the team with number seven front and center. The one and only Nicholas "Nick" Storvik, who had been her boyfriend then and was now her husband of sixteen years.

She felt his hands slip around her waist, smelled his cologne. He rested his chin on her shoulder. "Good memories, huh? Remember the infamous Mud Bowl? I scored a touchdown sliding the last ten yards, then went over to the sideline and picked you up to swing you around."

She laughed. "My mom was so mad. The dry-cleaning bill was atrocious."

He leaned over her shoulder to glance at the trophy, squeezed her waist. Their reflection stared back at them through the glass case. "Ever wish we could go back and do it all over again?"

She glanced down the hall, sighed. "Yeah, I do," she said.

But that was a lie. Because the truth was, for twenty years, she'd concocted most every excuse she could not to return to her hometown, and even after the few hours spent here today, she already sensed a desperate urgency to flee and never look back. And the long weekend was just beginning.

2

Reunited

They held the twenty-year class reunion at a venue known as the White Fence Farm, one of those local places popular for wedding receptions, milestone anniversaries, and special fundraisers. The decorating committee had graced the entrance with life size cardboard cutouts of the cast of *Friends* and *Seinfeld* with a couple of added empty spaces where you could poke your head through and add your face to the mix. Nick, dressed in pale-blue linen shirt and khaki slacks, saddled up next to Kramer, while Beth stood next to Elaine. The photographer took their picture and then they posed for a second with Joey and the gang. It was all a bit cheesy in Beth's mind, but what the hell? She needed to at least try and have fun.

Inside, the DJ had the nineties music spinning—Third Eye Blind, Barenaked Ladies—while guests signed in and wrote their names on tags so other classmates could identify them. Nobody wanted to be the one that had changed so much no one recognized them, unless, of course, they'd changed for the better—lost one hundred pounds or finally had plastic surgery on that nose that previously looked like the beak of a kiwi bird. Beth thought she and Nick had fared pretty well. She'd gained fifteen pounds, but the weight had distributed itself over her five-foot-five frame, and her hair had retained its natural blond. Nick had also gained some weight, and he was graying in the temples, but unlike many of his classmates, his hair was still thick and full, no receding hairline.

As the DJ played Chumbawamba, Beth and Nick left the registration table and headed inside where tables, decorated in their red and white school colors, surrounded a darkened dance floor speckled with disco lights. A group of guys huddled in the back near the bar began chanting, "Storv, Storv, Storv," the nickname the hometown crowd had used when cheering for Nick from the sidelines. Nick blushed and waved them off before quickly pretending to go back for a pass. The imaginary football went over the heads of the crowd, and one of his buddies imitated a run and catch before coming over and giving Nick a bro hug followed by a backslap. It took less than five seconds for Nick and Beth to be fully ensconced by former classmates.

Someone handed them both a beer.

"I'm so glad you two could make it. I thought maybe you'd moved to another country or something instead of Ohio," one of Nick's former teammates, Paul, teased. "You don't get back this way much?"

Beth sighed. She didn't know why their old classmates and friends always gave them a hard time about returning home. It wasn't as if they'd been gone entirely. They drove up to see Nick's parents at least once a year, and when big concerts hit Indianapolis or Detroit, they often met up with others and made a weekend out of it. Beth's parents had tired of the Michigan winters and had retired to Florida, so Beth and Nick had no other reason to come up to Michigan now other than to see Nick's family.

Nick shrugged. "Occasionally, Christmas mostly, a Michigan game or two. I always mean to arrange a get-together when we come up, but my parents tend to plan out every moment with us and the kids. The rest of the time they come to us. It's easier for the two of them to travel down to Ohio than it is for us to load up three kids and two dogs and venture this way. In fact, they're at our house now watching the kids while we're here since school has already started."

"Three?" Paul's wife said, poking her blond head into the party. She gave Beth a once-over. "Goodness, girl, you look great. How do you stay so petite? Fabulous dress too. Love the pink color and the off-the-shoulder look. My name is Wendy, by the way. Paul isn't too good on introductions. How old are your kids?"

"Will is thirteen, Jacob is nine, and my little girl, Anna, is five." Beth pulled out her phone, showed Wendy photographs of the kids, the ones she'd always known she would have with Nick. "Will is already as tall as Nick was in high school, and of course he's playing quarterback."

"A chip off the old block," Paul said, slapping Nick on the back again. "You still coaching the little ones?"

Nick nodded. "Pee wee football. Kids six to ten. It's great."

Beth had to show them a video of Jacob playing when he was younger, his helmet twice as big as his little body. "He kept running, but you can tell he can't see a thing through that gigantic helmet. Just tucked the ball under his right arm, held out his left to brush off tackles, and got those little legs running." The group laughed at the video of the kid who looked like a bobblehead doll on autopilot.

As the minutes wore on, they settled into various conversations, about kids and college, about what had and hadn't turned out as they'd expected. It was just as Beth had imagined it would be. Some classmates who'd been hugely popular in school had gone on to mediocre jobs and put their glory days behind them, while others who'd been near invisible in the school halls were now executives and entrepreneurs. Two classmates she remembered from her BPA days had teamed up to develop an iPhone app that had made them millionaires overnight, and another had started a business in Wisconsin that was now selling yogurt in every grocery store in America. A variety of successes and failures and lots of in-betweens, just as in life.

After finishing the first beer, Beth took a bathroom break, wondering why Joan hadn't yet arrived. Her best friend had promised her just the week before that she and her husband, Tom, would be attending. Although she and Joan had done well keeping in touch through college with regular weekend visits to each other's respective universities—Michigan State and Dayton—and had participated in each other's weddings, their visits since had diminished. Husbands, kids, and jobs—it was tough enough keeping up with your own circle without adding friends to the mix.

As Beth stopped at an outside mirror to refresh her lipstick, one shade darker than her dress, she heard a squeal from the other side of the room, then felt two arms wrap around her. She turned to see Joan's gray-green eyes and red-lipped smile. Her auburn hair still made her facial features light up like Christmas.

"I was beginning to wonder if you were going to make it," Beth said.

Joan waved a hand. "Ugh. Babysitter trouble. Nearly forty minutes late. See if I hire her again."

"Well, I'm really glad you're here. I was starting to get jittery. I mean, you know it's Nick who really wanted to come this weekend. I'm just trying to put on a happy face and get through it."

Joan put a hand on her hip. "Honey, why? I've never understood your hesitation to come back here. You and Nick were the most popular couple in our class. Everybody loves you here. You have nothing to be insecure about."

Beth grunted. "I don't know. I have nightmares. Like, Nick and I will be dancing and having a great time and *she'll* show up and ruin everything. Just like before."

"Good heavens, girl. That was so long ago. Besides, nobody ever believed those rumors anyway. Come on, let's find a table and catch up."

They grabbed two beers from the bar and settled in to talk. As Beth suspected, Joan made her feel better, but it didn't last. Soon, a few other former classmates joined them, including Lisa Berman, a tall, muscular blond who'd played volleyball and basketball in high school and was now a middle-grade PE teacher. Back in school, she'd been one of the biggest gossips, and that didn't appear to have changed.

"Will you look at Patty flirting over there with Bill? My God, she never gives up."

"Yeah, and he's eating it up," Joan said. "His wife looks like she's ready to claw his eyes out."

"I wonder how many couples end up in a fight when they return from a high school reunion?" Susan Beecher asked, now Susan Lewiski, after marrying Brett Lewiski, the designated class clown.

"About half, I'd guess," Lisa said.

"One of the very reasons I didn't want to come," Beth said, taking a large swill of beer.

"Oh, come on," Lisa said. "You and Nick? I can't imagine you two ever getting in a fight. I don't think I ever saw the two of you in high school when you weren't pawing each other."

She was right, of course. For the most part, Beth and Nick's relationship had been solid, even since high school. Sure, they had the occasional argument—mostly about how to discipline the kids or what major purchases to make—but they always made up before they went to bed. That was their rule. Never go to bed stewing all night over something that would seem menial by the next morning. They didn't have sex as often as they used to, but with three kids in the mix, who did? They were like every other couple—passing each other in the halls and out the door with a kid in tow on their way to a sports practice, game, or meeting with a teacher or coach. She hated that the only major face time they got was over a pillow after the nightly news, but she couldn't complain.

"I don't have to tell you, Beth. All the girls had the hots for Nick in high school," Lisa said, "but everyone knew he was taken. Nick Storvik was off-limits."

"Yeah, except that one girl. What was her name?" Susan asked, squinting to remember. "Melissa? Maria?" She snapped her fingers. "No, it was Missy. That was it."

Beth's stomach lurched. Here we go. Couldn't get through one night without *her*.

"Don't use her name," Joan said. She reached over and patted Beth's hand. "She gives Beth the heebie-jeebies. Beth here was worried she'd show up tonight and try to steal her man again—as if she'd ever had a chance—then or now."

Lisa broke out laughing. "Well, no worries on that one," she said. Lisa finished off the remaining wine in her glass before retrieving another from the bartender's tray.

"What do you mean?" Beth asked. "She was part of our class, albeit briefly."

"Yeah, but..." The smile fell from Lisa's face. "Oh my God, you haven't heard?"

Beth exchanged a glance with Joan. "Heard what?" Joan asked.

Lisa shifted in her chair. "Oh dear, you two really are out of touch," she said. Her eyes widened as she leaned across the table to whisper. "Turns out that rumor about Missy Ferguson running away after she had a fight with her parents? It wasn't true. Just a month ago, a construction crew found a body buried in the old wildlife preserve. Somebody dumped it there a long time ago via the surrounding marsh. Just last week, the authorities identified the bones as Missy Ferguson's. And, get this, they think she was murdered."

Joan gasped, pulled her hand back from Beth's, held it to her chest. "What?"

Lisa nodded. "Yes, our old classmate Jake Waters? He's Detective Jake Waters now, and he told me the autopsy indicated she died of something called blunt force trauma. It's been all over the news up here. What, do you people live in a bubble?"

"We live upstate now. I haven't heard of it," Joan said.

"And Nick and I are in Ohio," Beth said. "So, how and why would we know such a thing?"

Lisa sat back, placed her palms up, glanced at Joan. "I mean, I just figured..."

Beth squirmed. "You just figured because there was an old rumor about Missy and Nick that he would know something? Keep in touch with her family?"

Lisa waved her off. "No, of course not. I didn't mean to imply—"

"How did they find her anyway?" Susan interrupted. "Why was a construction crew in the wildlife preserve? It's state property. Protected property."

"The state sold some of the land," Lisa said. "Government money woes. They sold, like, one-third of the old preserve to a developer who wanted to build an apartment complex and a series of retail stores. They drained the marsh, filled it in, and started to build when...Missy turned up."

Beth sat back, stunned. Missy Ferguson was dead? She didn't know whether to be horrified or relieved, and immediately felt guilty for even thinking such a thing.

"How terrible for her and her parents," Beth said. "I mean, even though I didn't like the girl for obvious reasons, I would never wish her harm." She turned to Lisa. "Do they have a suspect?"

Lisa puckered her lips like a fish, looked uncertain if she should say what she was about to say. "Well, I don't know, but I would suspect if the parents and police believe any of those old rumors that Missy was pregnant when she disappeared, then you've got to believe they'll think the baby daddy is responsible."

Beth felt as if Lisa had slapped her across the face. A fire raced across her cheeks.

"Can they determine that from the body? If she was pregnant?" Joan asked, intervening before Beth could issue a tongue-lashing. Her friend still knew her well.

"And if so, can they determine the father? Like with DNA or something?" Susan followed.

Lisa shrugged. "Best ask Jake those questions." She motioned toward the entry, where a man, about six-two, with dark hair and even darker eyes, stood at the table shaking hands with other former classmates. Beth remembered him more as a biker type in high school, a motorcycle enthusiast who smoked in the parking lot and loved grunge music. Now, he looked a bit more urban cowboy, dressed in boots, jeans, and a sport coat.

As soon as the four of them glanced up, he turned their way and acknowledged their uninvited spying. A good detective knew when others were watching him, Beth guessed. She quickly scanned the crowd for Nick, saw him on the opposite side of the room laughing, and drinking a beer with another football teammate, one of the former linebackers. She wondered if she could intercept Nick and they could make a quick exit before Jake Waters had a chance to talk with him.

But it wasn't to be. As soon as Jake locked eyes on the duo, he excused himself from those nearby and began to maneuver toward the back—toward her husband, toward Nick Storvik.

The night had just turned into a nightmare.

3

Young Love

The first time Nick Storvik had kissed Beth McCallum he'd fallen in love. Some would tell him he was crazy, that at the age of fifteen he couldn't possibly have known what love was or what it felt like, but Nick would tell them they were wrong. He knew. The minute he'd nervously leaned over in the back row of that theater and felt those lips on his, he was toast. That kiss, so soft and innocent, might as well have created a custom seal pressed in wax and solidified for eternity. For the next hour, they'd sat in the back of that darkened movie house oblivious of their surroundings, kissing and cuddling.

He couldn't even remember the name of the movie.

He knew how dorky that sounded. He'd never confessed to his friends about his feelings, of course, the true intensity of his emotions for Beth McCallum. After all, he'd been the quarterback of the football team and had an image to maintain. Instead, he'd told the guys how he and Beth had made out for the entire show and bragged about how far he'd been able to get with her. That's what guys did. But it wasn't the truth.

It wasn't just her looks that had drawn him to her, although those were more than pleasing in and of themselves. Her fair skin, dark-brown eyes, and naturally red lips were the perfect study of contrast and contradiction, and, as he'd discovered the more they dated, mimicked the girl within. On one hand, Beth was every bit of the petite bubbly blond she demonstrated on the sidelines every weekend in her cheer uniform, reminding him of the champagne his parents drank every New Year's Eve. On the other hand, in private times, she could be smoldering and pouty, like a warm night's fire on a snowy night. One part port wine, one part brandy.

The other thing that had attracted Nick to her was her loyalty. To her friends, her family, and particularly, to him. Devotion didn't even seem to be an apt enough word to describe the level of commitment Beth McCallum held for people who endeared her. At times, it seemed more on the level of the worship or consecration one would have for a god or deity, but Nick couldn't deny he liked the attention. Every time he threw a touchdown, he'd peer over to the sidelines to see Beth waving her pom-poms or standing tall at the top of a pyramid so she could get a better look at him. They'd share a smile or a wink, the secret knowledge of their universal connection. Even the way she tumbled into the field at halftime, handsprings and turnovers, made him feel like she was doing it just for him. Flipping for Nick. Flipping over Nick.

The truth was, Beth McCallum looked upon him like no one else. It wasn't lust or invitation—those he received regularly—but pure admiration. When Beth focused on him, slid up beside him, and gave him a kiss, those lips might as well have been a chocolate bar. Smooth and creamy, with just a hint of sweetness. One he wanted to taste again and again and again.

That first summer at the end of their freshmen year, neither had owned a car yet, so they'd spent their days riding their bikes to the local parks where they hiked, swam, and generally hung out. On one occasion, they mastered a trail that took them to a secret cavern beneath a roaring waterfall where they'd found a rock to sit on and kissed until sunset. Nick could still remember the feel of her skin—cool and damp from the waterfall's spray—yet with a searing heat emanating beneath the surface. They sat there on that rock, both getting wet, and didn't care. Didn't have a care in the world, really.

Being together was all either of them needed or wanted.

At his baseball games, she'd ride up on her bike with her girlfriends, and they'd park outside the dugout. The coaches didn't like the distraction they presented to the players, but in truth, it got them pumped up. They liked to show off for the girls. Hit a little farther, throw a little harder, take a chance stealing second base.

Ah yes, second base. The first time Beth had let him slip his hands beneath her shirt he'd grown rock hard in an instant. They were French kissing by then, all sloppy tongues with absolutely no idea of what they were doing, but it didn't matter. They were in that adolescent time of exploration, discovering what felt good. When Beth had first sensed his erection, she'd groaned a little, turning him on even more, but had quickly pulled away. She'd said she was scared and wasn't ready, and begged Nick not to be angry with her. And, of course, he wasn't. Not then. Though maybe a little frustrated, his problem wasn't anything a cold shower couldn't fix. He told her he would wait until she was ready.

He just hadn't known then how much longer that would be.

It was around that time Nick's friends began to warn him that Beth's loyalty had evolved to an obsession. A crack appeared that summer in her personality, one of intense jealousy and rage. It started when a girl named Jennifer Dansen had come panting around him. A senior two years older with sultry dark eyes and a well-developed body, Jennifer's presence changed Beth from bunny to badger. On the surface, Beth appeared uncaring of her—unmovable behind a set of large sunglasses and lips as smooth as glass—but in moments of privacy, she'd lashed out at Nick with sharp teeth, tongue, and claws. He was never to see her, never to speak to her, else there would be consequences.

After catching Jennifer sidling up to Nick at his locker one day later that autumn, Jennifer Dansen had discovered the tires on her car slashed in the parking lot. No one knew who had done it, but Nick had a pretty good idea.

4

A Reckoning

The women around her kept talking, but Beth didn't hear a word they said. So many thoughts ran through her head, it was like she was listening to an entire orchestra play while everyone else only heard a violin. Five minutes later, Joan snapped her fingers in front of Beth's face to get her attention. "Earth to Beth..."

Beth blinked several times, realized both Lisa and Susan had departed. She glanced over to Nick's table again. Jake had made himself comfortable in a chair situated between Nick and the former linebacker, looking like a wolf anxiously awaiting to pounce on his prey. Joan followed Beth's gaze over her shoulder to check out what had Beth's attention before turning back.

She put her hand over Beth's, the one gripping her bottle of beer so hard her knuckles were white. "Look, I know you don't want to hear this," Joan said. "That was a bad time for you and Nick, but given the discovery of Missy and what has happened, Jake is going to have to talk to Nick. You know that."

Beth felt her mouth drop open, a rush of heat surface on her skin. "Not an hour ago you said no one believed those rumors. Why would you say that if you didn't believe it? Were you just saying that to placate me?"

"No, Beth, no. But just because no one believed them doesn't mean Missy didn't openly accuse Nick of getting her pregnant. I mean, you know that. You were there."

Beth pulled her hand away. "She was lying. She was always lying. Nick denied ever touching her." She shot Joan a look. "You think Nick was lying? You think Nick could hurt someone? You think Nick could *kill* someone?"

Her breaths emitted from her lungs in short, persistent gasps, as if she were about to hyperventilate. Behind Joan on the dance floor, five of their former classmates were lip-syncing to the Backstreet Boys. It should've been amusing, but all Beth could hear was her classmates' laughter, laughter directed not at the antics of the guys, but at her. Shocked. Surprised. Dazed.

And whispering. So much whispering.

Just like that day twenty-two years ago. When Missy had burst into the homecoming dance and accused Nick of the most unspeakable things. Blurted to the world that Nick Storvik had told her that he loved her, only to take her virginity and then leave her in a lurch when she told him she was pregnant.

Joan leaned over to make sure Beth locked in on those gray-green eyes of hers. "Honey, breathe. I'm not trying to insinuate anything about Nick. I know Nick would never hurt anyone. Jake just must do his job now and follow up with anyone who knew Missy. That includes Nick, and probably half of the people here tonight, including you and me. I'm sorry. I know you don't want to hear that. I know you don't want to go back to that time."

Beth glared at her best friend. *Don't want to go back?* That was an understatement. The truth was Missy Ferguson was the one and only reason Beth despised her hometown. All the good times she'd had at school, all the great days and nights spent on the lake and the football field, in class and out, they were all tainted now by the girl who'd come to town one summer and tried to take her boyfriend away. Even the places that had once occupied the most private of places in Beth's heart—like that spot in the woods she and Nick had first made love—was now tarnished forever. Stained by the memory of *that girl* pushing her way into their world and trying to pull them apart.

She glanced across the room at Nick, who was smiling and popping peanuts in his mouth while swigging his beer. Watched in horror as the former linebacker got up from the table and bid Jake and Nick a good night before joining another group nearby, leaving the two all alone.

Beth had to get over there. She had to intervene.

"I can't just sit here," Beth said. "I have to know what he's asking."

Joan started to object, but Beth was having none of it. She wasn't going to let someone accuse Nick willy-nilly based on innuendo and rumor. God knows he might've already had too much to drink and could say something that Jake could take the wrong way.

As she started toward the table, she saw her husband's face change as Jake broke the news to him. At first, his smile only faltered and his forehead tensed, leaving a ripple of concern between his eyebrows, but quickly, all former jovialness fell from him, as if he'd physically brushed it from his shirt. He shook his head, said something curt in response to one of Jake's questions. He glanced up and met his wife's eyes coming toward him across the room, could tell Beth was on a mission. He issued a slight shake of his head as if indicating for her to stop.

Beth halted, pulled the sheer ivory wrap she had draped across her bare shoulders a little closer. Behind her, she checked to see Joan's reaction, wondered if she should return to the table or forge ahead, but Joan was busy watching Nick too, analyzing his movements and reactions as if she were assuming the role of second detective.

Beth understood Nick's hesitancy to discuss Missy Ferguson in front of her, but this was one time she had to stand firm. She couldn't sit this one out. She wouldn't let *that girl* resurface these accusations against her husband—from the grave no less.

"Jake, hello," she said, coming up behind him and gripping his shoulder. He flinched at her unexpected touch, but smiled and stood to greet her.

"Beth, so good to see you."

They hugged before she moved to stand behind her husband. "You here by yourself?"

"Yes. My wife had to stay home with our new baby. She's just six weeks old."

"Congratulations," Beth said. "We have three ourselves. Anna, at five, is our youngest."

Jake nodded, gave a small smile. "That's great. No surprise there. You two always were inseparable."

He sure was good at keeping up appearances, Beth thought. She gathered that was yet another detective skill, showing no emotion. She turned toward Nick. "How come you're not out there lip-syncing and dancing with the rest of those goons?" she said, hoping to turn the conversation, and the night, away from the topic of Missy Ferguson. "Pretending to be the ultimate boy band. They look like they're having a great time. Probably be viral video stars tomorrow."

Nick took a swig of his beer, cocked his head. "Yeah, looks like fun," he said in a manner that indicated Jake had ruined any such chance of that happening.

The two exchanged hard stares.

"There's still time," Beth said. "For both of you."

"Maybe you should sit down, Beth," Jake said.

"No, you don't need to," Nick said. "Jake was just asking me—"

"Actually," Jake interrupted, "I'd like to speak with the both of you."

Nick stiffened.

Beth braced herself. So, there would be no escaping a discussion of *that girl*. She took a seat, huddled close to her husband. "So? What is it?"

Jake wrung his hands. They were exceptionally large, big enough to palm a basketball. "Well, unfortunately, I have a dual purpose in attending tonight's reunion. You remember a girl that went to our school junior year by the name of Missy Ferguson? She was only here for a short time, the summer and part of the fall 1996?"

Beth shot a glance at Nick, who flushed and looked at his lap. She could immediately sense the warmth that highlighted her cheeks as well, told herself to keep it cool. "Yes, of course I remember her, Jake, although I'd prefer not to, to tell you the truth," Beth said. "She did accuse my then-boyfriend of practically assaulting her." She rubbed Nick's arm to demonstrate her support for him. "Liar that she was, she still caused us a whole lot of trouble before she ran away."

Jake rolled the cap from his beer bottle back and forth across the table. "Yeah, well, about that... Turns out she didn't run away," he said.

Beth acted surprised. "No?"

"No. Her parents believed she'd run away because they'd had a terrible fight with their daughter just a few days before she went missing and there was no indication of foul play, but now...we know differently. She was murdered. Blunt force trauma to the back of her head, buried out in the preserve."

The fine hairs on the back of Beth's neck prickled. Even though it was the second time in under an hour she'd heard the news, the shock of it remained the same. "That's terrible," she said, a hand to her chest. "Do you think her parents were lying this whole time?"

He bit a lip. "Possibly. We're certainly looking into it, but...we have to look at all the options."

"Who else could it be?" Beth asked. "If the parents had a fight with their daughter a few days before, it makes sense it might've gotten out of hand and they tried to cover it up." She glanced at Nick. "Sounds like a *Dateline* episode."

She motioned to the waiter for another beer. Drank half.

When neither Nick nor Jake responded, she bounced her gaze from Nick to Jake, back to Nick. His unhappiness and discomfort were more than apparent. Beth pretended to just catch on. "Oh, come on, you can't be serious, Jake Waters. You suspect Nick? Because of that lie Missy told everyone?" She leaned in, shook a wayward finger at him. "Let me tell you something. If Missy was pregnant—and that's a big if— that baby was not Nick's baby."

Nick slouched.

Jake raised his hands, fending off the tirade that was sure to come. "Listen, I don't mean to cause a rift between you two. I don't. If you'd rather come down to the station..."

"Oh, hell no," Beth said. "Nick is not going to the police. That's ridiculous."

Jake took a deep breath. "Then I'm sorry, but I have to ask." He shifted his attention away from Beth. "Nick, did you ever have sex with Missy Ferguson?"

Beth closed her eyes. The all too familiar bomb of jealousy exploded in her chest. Affronted, slighted, disrespected. Just like the night of the homecoming dance and for weeks afterward, when the humiliation followed, dark and thick. And later when...

What? Beth couldn't remember. But she remembered feeling the same—ready to detonate.

Nick started to answer Jake's question when Beth interrupted. "Was she?" she asked.

"Was she what?" Jake asked.

"Pregnant?"

He sighed. "I'm not sure we'll ever know," Jake said. "Obviously, the body has decomposed. There was nothing but bones left. Depending on how far along she was, there could be evidence, but it might be difficult to determine. Right now, the medical examiner is looking for those answers."

Beth took another guzzle from the beer, wiped away the liquid that escaped down her chin. "Sorry to sound uncaring, but it seems pointless then for Nick to answer your question. You will have a very tough time proving anything Missy Ferguson said was something other than a total lie. The girl was just...trouble."

Jake leaned back and examined her. He didn't look happy. "Well, that's why I need to talk to everyone who knew her. See if they heard or saw anything suspicious around the time she went missing. The police didn't do much back in the days she disappeared, so we're relying on some pretty fuzzy memories."

Beth started to speak again, but Nick's squeeze of her hand told her to be quiet.

He spoke up. "Look, Jake, we're not here to impede any investigation. We know you have a job to do. This is what I can tell you. I never touched Missy Ferguson. She had a crush on me, yes, and she tried to get me to...you know. But when I said no, she got angry. Revenge angry. That's when she came at me and Beth during the homecoming dance. I don't have to tell you how embarrassing that was for me, and for Beth."

"So, you never had sex with her?"

Nick flushed, brushed unseen lint from his pants. "No, of course not."

Jake paused. "Okay." He said it in a long, stretched out way that made it clear he thought Nick was lying, scribbled a little notation in his book that Beth couldn't see. She didn't like that.

"After Missy alleged Nick got her pregnant, you attacked her the night of the dance, isn't that right?" he asked without giving Beth the courtesy of a glance.

Beth grimaced. She turned away, hating to relive one of her less-than-finest moments. After Missy had announced her situation to the world, the entire dance had come to a halt, with everyone circling around Nick and Beth and Missy, all waiting to see how Nick would take the news and Beth would react. And react, she had. Beth hadn't taken kindly to the girl interrupting her homecoming dance with her future husband—practice for their future wedding—and accusing him of such an atrocity. Beth had pounced on Missy Ferguson and was pulling her hair and punching her face before she knew what hit had her. "Yes, but Jake, she lied."

Jake scratched a few more notes on his little pad. "Other than the fight between you and Missy at the homecoming dance, was there ever another time you two had a confrontation?"

Beth pretended to think. There had been an earlier incident at the clinic, when Beth had been awaiting her birth control pills and Missy had come charging out from a back room, a doctor trailing behind her. Missy had been beyond distraught, crying while the doctor pleaded for her not to do anything drastic. Missy had caught sight of Beth sitting there and stopped cold with her hands on her stomach, as if trying to conceal the truth from her rival Beth McCallum. It had been in that moment—a full two months before the homecoming incident—when they'd exchanged the glance that left them both knowing the truth.

But Jake didn't need to know about such details. And neither did her husband. She'd kept that encounter secret a long time and planned for it to remain that way.

Beth shook her head. "No, never."

"Did either of you encounter Missy the following two weeks after homecoming?"

Beth and Nick shared a glance. "I think the last time we saw her was at the lake. It was one of those rare Indian summer days in mid-October. Sometime afterward, she just...disappeared. Never showed up for school again," Nick said.

Jake sighed. "Okay, anything else you can tell me that might help?"

They both shrugged. "I mean, it's like you said," Nick said, "Memories are fuzzy at best. But we'll certainly call you if either of us remembers anything."

"Well, thank you for your information. Enjoy the rest of your evening." Finally, he stood to leave.

When he was gone, Beth let out a huge sigh of relief. She let go of Nick's arm, only to see a deep imprint left in his skin. She hadn't realized just how hard she'd been hanging on to him. She rubbed the area, examined her husband. The conversation with Jake Waters had sobered him up. He glanced around the crowd nervously, like a chicken in a coop. Nick Storvik, suspected baby daddy, suddenly didn't look much like Nick Storvik, confident athlete. Instead, he resembled a man who was already under suspicion for the murder of Missy Ferguson.

Beth took note of the several sets of eyes upon them, the sideways glances, the silent whispers, and felt transported right back to that dance so many years ago. And suddenly, she wanted to leave.

Why, oh, why couldn't Missy Ferguson just have stayed in her cold dark grave?

5

Pressure

The day started off with a two-mile run on a path beside the lake. It was a cool, foggy morning at the cheerleading camp in mid-Michigan, where Beth would spend the next week learning new routines with other girls from across the state. Running had never been her thing, so she stuck with the middle of the pack, jogging at a mild pace. It wasn't that she didn't have the stamina to run faster, she just found the constant one-foot-in-front-of-the-other routine boring. She preferred recreation that challenged the body and the mind into learning new skills and movements, like gymnastics and dance, although she also enjoyed rowing, which she supposed tapped into the same strong mental focus and rhythm needed as competitive running. The constant pounding of feet on the pavement, like the repetitive row of the oar, relaxed her mind and cleared away the clutter in a way that allowed her to think about things that were troubling her. Sometimes these things were nothing more than what to wear to an upcoming party or deciphering the true meaning of something somebody had said, but today, it was far more serious matter—sex.

And in particular, sex with Nick.

The night before, she'd stayed up late with the girls, huddled in their respective beds but continuing to talk across the dark cabin, when the discussion had turned to first times and losing their virginity. With great intensity, Beth had listened as girl after girl told of their first encounters, teenagers grinding and bumping in the night. When it was Beth's turn to share, the others were surprised to hear that she was still a virgin, given her long-standing relationship with Nick. They'd all been certain that Beth and Nick must've consummated their relationship long ago since they were going on two years dating, and they couldn't believe someone as handsome as Nick Storvik was a virgin as well. They all warned her that she'd better think about putting out soon as there was no way he would wait much longer.

And Beth knew they were right. Over the past few months, Nick had grown increasingly frustrated about their lack of progress in the sex department. It had been nearly a year since the first time she'd allowed him to feel her up and rub her in other places with her clothes still on, but they still hadn't gone all the way, and it was making him crazy. Although they'd come close several times, Beth always put the brakes on at the last minute.

For the past two months, since she'd turned sixteen, he'd been steadily upping the pressure. He told her that he was ready, more than ready, and that he loved her. Their first time wouldn't be like all the others she'd heard about, squirming and uncomfortable, or painful and unpleasant. Nick assured her they would make love, and he would be gentle. Others their age were doing it regularly, and Nick didn't want to miss out on the experience. Obviously, she wanted her first time to be with Nick, and she didn't want sex—something that should bring them closer—to be the thing that came between them. So, after discussing it at length one night, Beth and Nick decided that they would have sex for the first time on the Fourth of July this year. After the lighted parade of boats was over, they'd stay out late and find an empty cabin near the lake and do it. Fireworks of a whole different kind.

The following week, she'd gone to the clinic to get on the pill. The doctor had told her it could take up to two months to be effective, so to be cautious and use extra protection for a time. She said it was a good idea anyway because of STDs that caused all kinds of rashes, breakouts, and itching. Beth had blushed at that, not really wanting to talk about such terrible things. She told the doctor that she and Nick would never have that problem, because she and Nick would only be with each other—now and forever.

She hadn't really liked the little head tilt and lip curl the doctor had offered in return.

Beth listened to her footsteps pound the trail, a *whump, whump, whump* of feet that reminded her of drumbeats. She imagined what their first time would be like, the cabin flickering with low candlelight, the remaining spark of a campfire outside, the window open to let in the lightest breeze. The curtains would softly billow inward as he would lay her down, caress her cheek, kiss her full on the mouth. Slowly, he would slip his hands beneath her shirt and slide it up and over her head, then...

Before she knew it, she got lost in the moment and forgot all about the run.

The two miles were nearing completion as the sun poked through the fog and cast its rays through the treetops, highlighting the dew that remained. As Beth rounded up the final hill, her right ankle caught the root of a tree that had upended in the path and she went down, hard. She grunted as she landed, her lungs inhaling a fistful of dirt as her head hit the trail. She sat up and wiped herself off, spit dirt, looked at her ankle. It was already swelling. She almost burst out laughing realizing what her sex dreams had just done to her.

Two girls stopped to help her up and assisted her back to the main cabin where a nurse checked her out. Two hours later, the nurse informed Beth she wouldn't be participating in any more cheerleading camp festivities. Instead, she was to limit the pressure on her ankle for at least one week and was to see a doctor immediately if she experienced any change in vision or sudden headaches. The other girls were disappointed to lose one of their team, but secretly Beth was thrilled. Although she'd only spent five days at camp, she was already counting down the days until she could return home and see Nick. She missed him terribly.

And now, with no reason to be here, she could leave early and go home.

She bit her bottom lip. Maybe they wouldn't have to wait until the Fourth of July after all.

Nick was camping with the guys right now. With many of the girls away, the guys had rented a couple of cabins on the lake and would be enjoying their first week in June water-skiing and spending nights around the campfire telling stories of their own. Which meant Nick had access to a cabin right now they could use, if they were so inclined.

That was it. She decided it was time.

She packed her things and told the girls what she was planning to do. They all squealed and offered various bits of advice. She got in the family car she'd driven up to the camp, having just gotten her license weeks before, started up the engine, and smiled at herself in the rearview mirror. First her period, then her license, and now, this. She was beginning to feel like a real adult.

And by morning, she hoped to be one step closer to being a woman.

6

A Surprise

B ack at the hotel they'd reserved for the long weekend, Beth readied herself for bed. She kicked off her high heels and slid free of the pink sheath dress she wore. She removed her makeup and washed her face, then pulled her hair free of the tangled updo she'd created for the reunion. After taking a quick shower, she wiped the steam from the mirror and took a good, hard look at herself. The fine lines beneath her eyes were more tensed than usual, and an unknown soul looked back at her through those brown eyes. *Who are you?*

She hated the way she always got so angry and defensive when anyone brought up Missy Ferguson. Nick had told them long ago that Missy's accusations weren't true, and he'd reiterated that same message tonight. So, why couldn't they just believe him and leave it alone?

She'd hated the way Jake had accusingly asked him that fateful question.

I have to ask... Did you ever have sex with Missy Ferguson?"

Her husband had hidden his face in the same manner as when his parents had asked him that question that long-ago summer. And Beth had experienced that slap of humiliation again, once more facing her boyfriend's alleged infidelity. But it wasn't Nick she was angry with so much as Jake, and why he'd felt the need for airing such a matter—their dirty laundry—at a public event. Couldn't he have waited until the reunion was over? Reunions were supposed to be about reminiscing the good times— the games, the parties, the fun times in class. Not discussing a former classmate discovered dead in the wildlife preserve. No one wanted to think about that. No one wanted to think about *her.*

Least of all Beth.

Damn you, Missy Ferguson, why couldn't you just stay dead?

She frowned at herself. What an awful thing to think. Yet, she couldn't help it. It had taken years to forget the memories of that summer and fall and now everything was resurfacing, even Missy herself, straight from the grave. As if she knew Nick and Beth would have to return to their hometown this year and she was determined to make her voice heard again.

Beth hated it, having to relive it.

She thought about how she'd been so excited leaving cheerleading camp that night to surprise Nick. She'd driven back home in record time, arriving just before sunset. Beth had found out from other friends at the lake where Nick and the guys were camping and had taken a row-boat out to the area. As she'd rowed, the sun had gradually disappeared from the horizon and the night had come to life, the lightning bugs thick as stars in the sky flashing green and yellow, the bullfrogs croaking, the night herons calling nearby. She distinctly remembered the soft splash the rows made in the water, the oars turning in their locks. *Swoosh, crank, swoosh, crank.* It was a soothing, calming sound, especially in the dark.

When she'd arrived, she'd hoisted the boat up to the sandy shore before walking the barely visible trail through the marshy grassland that led to the cabins, careful to keep the bulk of her weight off her bad ankle. As she approached the area, Beth could see several guys in the distance sitting around a campfire, but Nick wasn't among them. Not wishing to announce her arrival to his friends and ruin the surprise, she avoided them and hiked up the slight incline to where the cabins sat overlooking the lake. She went from cabin to cabin peeking through the mostly darkened windows when she came upon one with a soft flickering light and curtain billowing inward. She thought back to the daydream she'd had that morning before she'd gone down on the trail and knew it had to be the one.

She made her way to the window, favoring her gimpy ankle, and looked in.

Beth had come all this way to surprise her boyfriend, but he wasn't the one who'd gotten the surprise. Instead, it was Beth, who'd arrived to find a naked Missy Ferguson standing before Nick like the devil incarnate. She'd cornered him there in the cabin all alone and stripped off all her clothes, then invited him to touch her in places no one had touched her before. And although Nick had appeared hesitant, touch her he had.

All while Beth stood outside watching the entire thing unfold.

It was just as Beth had imagined—except she wasn't the girl lying under Nick Storvik.

The emotions that had flowed through Beth at that time were like a torrential storm—rain, thunder, and lightning coming in the form of tears, cries, and fist-pounding. Heartbreak, yes, but also a level of hatred and jealousy the likes of which Beth couldn't fathom. The images before her were too much to bear—the arch of Missy's back, the wrap of her long legs around Nick's torso, the soft thrusts of his pelvis. Forever now imprinted upon her mind like scenes from a bad movie, except it was real.

For nearly two years, she and Nick had been waiting for the perfect time, but now she, Beth, would not be his first. It was, and would always be Missy Ferguson, and that enraged Beth with an intensity she never knew she could feel. It had been the first time she blacked out—an experience that would recur from time to time throughout her life—when life's stresses and pressures became overwhelming and her brain simply seized and locked down. A few minutes later, Beth snapped from her daze and saw the two of them lying there, covers pulled waist high, Nick face-down while Missy ran her fingers across his back.

Then, voices approaching, the guys heading up to the cabins from the campfire below, and Missy and Nick scrambling to dress and sneak away before the guys discovered them. And Beth had taken off through the brush, lumbering as best she could to get back down the hill and through the marshy grasses until she'd reached the boat and rowed back to shore before driving home through a blur of tears and heartache.

And Nick didn't know she knew, not to this day.

It still made her so angry that, there in the quietness of the hotel bathroom, she slammed her fist, and the mirror in her hand, down on the counter and shattered it into a thousand pieces. She felt, more than saw, the glass and plastic splinter and graze across her knuckles, heard pieces clatter to the floor, realized how loud it all sounded.

"Beth?" she heard Nick say from the room. "You okay?"

She glanced at herself in the mirror, shook her head, realized she had temporarily blacked out again, just as she'd done on that night so many years ago. She observed the face staring back at her—furious, outraged, blood pulsing—knew she needed to pause for a moment, get herself together. She couldn't let Nick see her this way.

She took several deep breaths and practiced her mantra of pushing the images of Missy Ferguson away. Ten minutes later, she'd gathered herself enough to join him in the bedroom. She flicked off the lights in the suite so he wouldn't be able to see her full face, just in case any hint of her former expression remained.

Nick lay on the bed, naked except for his boxer shorts, basking in the glow of the television. His eyes concentrated on the screen before him, but she could see he wasn't really engaged, his pupils cast distantly and shifting ever so slightly, indicating his thoughts were elsewhere. "What broke?" he asked.

"My hand mirror," she said. "It slipped right from my hand and landed face down on the corner of the vanity. I think I found all the glass, but don't go in their barefoot." She rounded the bed, pulled the covers down, slipped in between the sheets.

"Does breaking a hand mirror still equate to seven years bad luck?" Nick asked.

"I hope not." She fluffed a pillow, then two, sat up against them.

For the next twenty minutes, silence sat between them like a newly arrived stranger.

"That was a little unnerving tonight, huh?" Nick said.

Beth closed her eyes. Ran her hands along her shivering arms.

"You want to talk about it?" he asked.

She shook her head.

The fine lines around his eyes twitched. "You don't believe..."

"No, of course not," she said, maybe too quickly. "You told me nothing happened. I believe you. It's crazy he would suspect you. I'm sure we were together during the time she disappeared."

He shot her a glance from the corner of his eye. Nodded along with her. "That's right."

She slid under the covers, rolled over, and gave him a kiss before turning out the reading light. Behind her, Nick did the same and turned off the television as well, until they both lay there in the darkness, back to back.

Yes, Nick had been with Beth. Nick had been with her at the lake and hadn't been anywhere near that wildlife preserve then or in the following weeks after Missy disappeared. She was certain of it.

Yet, the thing was—that wasn't entirely true. The truth was, Beth McCallum couldn't remember anything that happened the last two weeks of October 1996 at all.

7

Seduction

N ick lay in the dark room, thinking about the cold, decaying body of Missy Ferguson. For twenty-two long years, she'd stayed in her shallow grave waiting for someone to find her. He imagined the type of animals and preserve life that had discovered her first and stripped the rotted flesh from her bones, fathomed the variety of insects that had nested and laid eggs, turning her body into their maternal playground. When she was about to be a mother herself, the mother of Nick's child.

The thought of that reality now haunted him. Had a child—his child—died the day Missy Ferguson had died? She'd shown him the pregnancy test, the clinical results, but he'd been in denial about the outcome. They'd only slept together that one night, just that single time, and he couldn't believe a brief hour could possibly produce consequences that could control and destroy the rest of his life. It was unfathomable to think sheer seconds could turn his whole life upside down.

Missy Ferguson had first arrived in town in the spring of 1996, just a few weeks before school was due to end for the year. Her father had taken the position of pastor for the New Life Presbyterian Church just east of town, having moved his family here from his prior position near Lansing. Like Beth, Missy was fair-skinned, but tall, with legs that seemed to go on forever and flowing dark hair that extended halfway down her back. The first time Nick had seen her, he'd been at the lake sailing with his friends, on a rare occasion when Beth hadn't been present. Beth's maternal grandmother had passed away the week before, and her parents had insisted she come with them to Florida for the funeral.

He remembered his first encounter with Missy vividly. As he sat shirtless on the side of a sailboat, he and his entourage passed her on the shore. She was doing her best Daisy Duke impression, wearing denim cutoffs and a bikini top, while leaning against the side of the concession stand. It wasn't so much that Nick had been interested in her, but not to look at the beautiful piece of artwork that was Missy Ferguson would've been unnatural. Even without knowing a thing about her, Nick could sense her rebellious nature, emanating between the puffs of smoke leaving her lips as she drew on the cigarette in her hand and the single button left unfastened on her shorts.

Nick's best friend, Paul, navigating the boat, nearly crashed into a dock ogling her. "Who is that?" he asked, lowering his sunglasses to get a better look.

"I've never seen her before," another friend, Louis, said. "Believe me, I'd remember."

"Me too," Nick said. He issued a slight nod toward her from the boat. With her eyes hidden behind large sunglasses, he wasn't sure she saw him until she flicked her ashes and returned the gesture. Such was the day their relationship began.

Later, when the sun was going down, Nick and the gang tied up the sailboat and settled by the lakeshore for the evening. Although the day had been unusually warm for mid-April in Michigan, the evening cooled considerably, so they huddled around a campfire in shorts and sweatshirts. Nick felt unusually lonely, having no girlfriend to cuddle and kiss, and went to the concession stand to get a couple of burgers. There, Missy stood nearby. She'd been the one to start the conversation.

"Those your homeboys?" she asked.

Nick laughed. "You could say that."

"You look a little lonely. No girlfriend?"

"She's out of town."

Missy ran a finger down his arm. "That's too bad. You want some company?" She nodded over her shoulder at an older model Subaru. "I've got the car for the evening. Maybe we can go for a ride?"

He glanced at Missy, back at the boys. They paid him no attention, too engrossed with talk and laughter and the girls on their laps. "Sure, why not?" So, with the excuse that he was tired and heading home, he walked up an adjoining road, circled around, and waited for Missy Ferguson to pick him up in her car. They drove around for a couple of hours then parked at a secluded spot, where they ended up making out.

He should've left it alone after that first encounter. He should've walked away. But he didn't.

The girl was relentless in her pursuit of him over the next few weeks. At school, she'd wink at him in the halls or slip him a secret note, asking him to meet her. She'd trap him by the lockers and whisper in his ear. It didn't take long for the rumors to fly. That's when Beth began asking questions, wanting to know what was going on. Nick always gave her the same response. "Nothing."

Beth started getting paranoid. Worried Missy would appear around every turn and needle her way in the minute Beth wasn't around, she became even more clingy than usual, until Nick started to feel the choking suffocation his friends had long-warned him about. Worse, Nick was growing hornier by the day and Beth wasn't providing any relief. Nick was almost seventeen. Beth had just turned sixteen. He understood they were still young, but they'd been together for nearly two years and yet, she had him waiting. And truth be told, he was sick and tired of it.

Then came June. Beth had gone to cheer camp for ten days and Missy knew he'd be alone. So, every day for five days in a row, she'd come to the lake, parading around in a thong bikini that left little to the imagination. Pouty breasts begging to be fondled, her entire ass cheeks on display for the world to see. Nick got hard just watching her walk past. The college guys up from Ann Arbor took notice too, and took turns offering her rides on their boats and Jet-Skis, but as guy after guy approached, each walked away disappointed. For whatever reason, she only had eyes for Nick Storvik.

He felt like a prized rooster the new hen was parading around.

One night, after a full day of water-skiing on the lake, he'd left the campfire and walked up the hill to one of the cabins to retrieve a couple more beers they kept in a cooler there. Because they were all underage, he had to pour them into Styrofoam cups. He popped the tops and filled four cups, and as he turned to leave, he saw Missy Ferguson standing there in the cabin. She was leaning in the doorway with her arms crossed, blocking the exit.

"Can I get one of those?" she asked.

Nick felt cornered, but simply shrugged. "Of course." He found another cup, rummaged through the ice for a cold can. By the time he turned around a second time, she was standing directly in front of him. Her nipples were erect beneath her shirt, the result of the cool night air and no bra.

"I need to take these out to the guys," he said. "You want to join us?"

She took a long pull on the beer. "Not really. I'd rather stay here and get comfortable." She ran that deadly finger down his arm once again, the same one that had caused him to make a bad decision before. Just her touch turned him on. "Will you come back?" she asked.

He glanced over his shoulder, back at Missy. This was his moment of truth. If he was going to finally lose his virginity, he could do it now or wait another month for Beth. They had decided upon the Fourth of July, which wasn't that far away, yet, he feared she might change her mind once again. He wouldn't get another opportunity like this. The guys were down below and hadn't likely seen Missy come up the hill from the other direction. He could take them the beer to keep them occupied, then return and have total privacy.

Sensing his indecision, she inched closer and leaned her breasts into his chest, took her hand and lightly brushed over the bulge between his legs. An involuntary moan escaped his throat. She smiled, pleased.

"I'll be right back," Nick said.

When he returned, she'd stripped down to nothing but her underwear. Just walked around naked in the glow of the candlelight, her pale skin illuminated and long, dark hair flowing freely down her back. She came over to him and asked him if he wanted to get out of his shorts. And what was he to do? A healthy, vibrant seventeen-year-old boy dealing with urges he didn't yet know how to contain?

He shut the door and closed the curtains, his breaths as rapid as his heartbeat with the anticipation of what was to come. With legs splayed open, she motioned him over to the bed and invited him to touch her. Told him to kiss her. Demanded that he taste her. Then, at last, he felt what it was like to be inside a woman.

And after that night, Nick Storvik's life had never been the same.

8

Row, Row, Row Your Boat

Today, the committee had scheduled part two of the reunion to take place on the lake, a day filled with water-skiing, volleyball, and picnics. Beth wondered how late the party had lasted the night before and how those who'd over indulged would look and feel today. She, for one, was looking forward to a better day. Hopefully, everyone had shared their secrets and gossip and gotten it all out of their system so Nick and Beth could have some peace.

Beth hadn't gotten much sleep, and Nick had fared little better, tossing and turning most of the night. He blamed it on the poor air-conditioning in the room, but Beth suspected there might be more to it. She'd often wondered if he'd known Missy was pregnant and considered whether he had another child out there somewhere he didn't know about. After last night, he now knew with certainty that wasn't true. If Missy Ferguson had been pregnant when she'd died, then his child had died right along with his mother.

How would that make him feel? Sorrow? Relief? Did he ever think about what his life would've been like if he'd married Missy instead of Beth?

Beth felt her eyes narrow. *Why do I keep doing this? Torturing myself with memories of Missy?* Once again, she took a moment to rid herself of the images of *that* girl.

After putting the final touches of her makeup on, she grabbed her cell phone, sat on the edge of the bed while Nick showered, and rang the kids. She hadn't checked in the prior night and wanted to see how things were going with them.

The phone rang twice before Will answered. "Hi, Mom."

"Hi, baby. How are things? Grandma and Grandpa spoiling you?"

"Yes. We went to Skyline last night."

Skyline was a Cincinnati legend. They served up chili with spaghetti, cheese, and onions, and other than the single-slice cheese pizza at Kings Island, it was Will's absolute favorite food.

"How was the first night of the reunion?" he asked.

"Crazy," she said truthfully. "But you'll be glad to know that neither of us ended up dancing with a lampshade on our head."

"I hope you weren't dancing at all. The last thing I want my friends to see is my parents on You Tube."

"Hey, I'm a very good dancer. You're father?" She glanced over at Nick, who was standing in the doorway drying himself with a towel. He raised an eyebrow. "Well, he did play a bit of air guitar last night. Got his Eddie Vedder on."

"Who's that?" Will asked. "Does he rap?"

Beth shook her head. It was generation-fail times like these that she realized just how much had changed in twenty years. It only felt like a minute had passed since high school, yet every day she had three kids to remind her of how much time had truly gone by.

She spoke to Jacob and Anna briefly, then blew kisses into the phone and hung up. Afterward, she turned to Nick, now shaved, and dressed. "Our kid doesn't know who Eddie Vedder is. Tell me again, when exactly did we get old?"

Nick laughed, promised Will was just pulling her strings. "I play plenty of Pearl Jam in the car. He can't escape it, although maybe he'd like to. If I must listen to the likes of some rapper-of-the-moment I've never heard of or can't understand, he has to suffer my vices too."

"One day it's Bubble Guppies and Henry Hugglemonster, and the next thing you know they're dancing hip-hop and wearing their pants too low." Beth sighed. "If Anna starts twerking anytime soon, that's going to be the end of it."

Nick kissed her on the cheek. "Come on, we're going to be late."

Now noon, they drove to the lake and met up with the other on-time arrivals. Before they got out of the car, they gave each other a glance, a look that said they both just wanted to have a good day and forget all the insinuations Jake Waters had made the night before. Beth planned to follow the plan, but also resolved to give Jake a private lashing and a piece of her mind if he showed up today, for having ruined what had started out to be such a perfectly good evening the night before.

How dare he suspect my husband of something so heinous as murder.

As they approached the gathering, everyone greeted them enthusiastically, although Beth sensed something amiss, as if those present had just been talking about them. "How'd you sleep, sweetie?" Joan asked.

"Fine, considering I'm in a strange bed," Beth lied.

"Nick too?" she asked, squinting into the bright sun.

Beth forced a smile. "Snored like a baby."

"Good to hear," Joan said, matching one fake smile with another before grabbing a bowl of potato salad and removing the plastic covering. Beth chipped in to help, adding serving utensils to pans of baked beans and various other side dishes. Nick joined the guys near the grill, who were flipping burgers and hot dogs. As Beth and the women chit-chatted, she tried not to imagine the real thoughts and questions the women standing before her were thinking in their inquiring little minds. Were Missy's allegations against Nick all those years ago true? Was Missy truly pregnant with his baby? And most of all, was it possible Nick Storvik was a murderer?

It took lunch and a half a case of beer until someone decided to broach the subject aloud. To no one's surprise, it was Lisa Berman. "Jake Waters sure made the rounds last night, didn't he? Poking his nose in places it doesn't belong. He even had the nerve to ask me if I ever got into a fight with Missy Ferguson or knew who else did."

She shook her head at Beth, made a little face. "Ridiculous, right?"

Beth wanted to punch her lights out.

Joan piped in. "I told Jake he should probe a little deeper into Missy's parents, especially her father. If you ask me, it makes perfect sense. They admitted to having a fight with her days before. Who's to say things didn't get out of hand?"

"But he's a preacher," another woman exclaimed, hand to her chest.

"Precisely," Joan said. "A preacher with a congregation who might not take kindly to an unwed pregnant daughter. Trust me, stranger things have happened. You know her upbringing was likely a key reason for her behavior. Suppressed by strict, religious parents. She was rebelling."

Joan's husband, Tom, nodded as he continued to shove potato chips into his mouth. "Not like parents haven't killed their kids before," he mumbled. "I've certainly wanted to kill mine a couple of times."

Joan slapped his arm. "Stop that."

"The parents never mentioned foul play, and why would they if they did it?" Lisa said. "Why force the police to look for something you're trying to cover up?"

Another woman, mousy with graying hair, nodded. "You could be right," she said. "They kept pleading for Missy to come home but never once suspected something else might've happened to their daughter? That's suspicious to me."

Joan finished off her beer and twisted the cap from another. Beth's friend was taking full advantage of her time away from the kids. "Well, I know one thing. It was ridiculous for Jake to interrogate Nick like that last night. All that innuendo from twenty-two years ago. Jake swears nothing happened between him and Missy, and I believe him." Joan winked at Beth, a sign of support.

"Not to mention he was with me the entire weekend she supposedly disappeared, so there's absolutely no reason to suspect him," Beth interjected, hearing the defensiveness in her tone. She popped the cap from a second brew of her own, drank one-third of it.

All those seated around the table nodded. Of course, they would agree with her—Nick's wife—while she was sitting here among them. She turned to see Nick standing at the next picnic table, spooning baked beans, and appearing uncomfortable with the conversation.

One of the husbands intervened. "Hell, the only thing Nick Storvik is capable of killing is a thirty-yard pass down field," he said, his ample beer belly juggling beneath a too-tight T-shirt. "So, what do you say, Nick? Little game of touch football after we eat?"

After lunch, the guys picked teams round-robin style and started to play. Beth hung back with many of the women, popping another round of beers. Halfway in, the tongues began to wag again.

"What the hell would Missy be doing out at the preserve anyway? Nothing but forest and marsh land," a classmate Beth couldn't name, and only remembered from a shared algebra class, said.

"Well, she probably didn't go out there by herself. There weren't even roads into some of that land back then. Some places you could only get to by boat," Lisa Berman chimed in.

"Got to hand it to somebody," a brash woman by the name of Laura said. "Good place to bury a body. They were smart enough to bury it up on the land and not leave it swimming in the marsh. Somebody surely would have found or seen a floater."

"I don't know," Lisa followed. "Think of all the critters in those waters. Might not take long before there would be nothing left to discover."

A small, petite lady with spiky jet-black hair cringed. "Please, we just ate."

"I feel bad for her," Susan Lewiski said. "Just because she was a bit rebellious against her parents and loose with the guys didn't mean she deserved to die."

"I don't think she was loose," Lisa said. "She flirted, but she really only had eyes for Nick. I heard Nick was her first..." Lisa stopped and stared wide mouthed at Beth once again, the second time in as many days she'd publicly affronted her.

Seriously, didn't this woman know how to keep her mouth shut?

Beth had had enough. She couldn't take it anymore. These women were like an entire row of those horrible little dolls that repeat the same phrases over and over every time you pulled their string. And they wouldn't shut up. They just couldn't for one single moment close their ridiculous little mouths.

She slammed her fist upon the table, making the silverware jump and a couple of plastic cups tip over. One woman gave out a little yelp before—at last—they shut up. "It doesn't matter what people say, or think, or speculate, because I know the truth. My husband didn't cheat with Missy Ferguson. My husband had nothing to do with her death. My husband is not capable of harming another human being. Now, can we *please* change the subject?"

34

Behind them, they briefly heard the game come to a halt. Somebody's husband asked if everything was okay. They all waved and nodded until the men returned to football.

Amid an awkward silence, Susan cleared her throat and started gathering used paper plates and cups and taking them to the trash. Several others followed. Joan remained seated across from her best friend. "Right on," she said, giving Beth a little fist bump.

The other women turned their attention to the game at hand and cheering for their husbands. Beth remained at the table, hidden behind her sunglasses and simmering a slow, roiling boil. *Nick, this. Nick, that. Missy, Missy, Missy. Poor dead girl Missy.*

Across the lawn, she watched as the center hiked the ball toward Nick, observed him going back and arching his arm, then extending a long pass down to a running man in cargo shorts. Smiled as he caught up to an opponent and tagged him before the guy even knew he was present. Athletic, agile Nick, such a good catch.

So, why did Beth hate him so much at this moment?

You know why, her conscience nagged. *Because he did it. He slept with Missy Ferguson.*

She stood. "I'm going for a row."

"What?" Joan gave her a funny look. "Are you sure? You've had, like, three beers," she said, her own words slurring, *three* coming out like *tree.*

Beth waved off her concerns, trotted down to the lake. Other than cheerleading, and the gymnastics and tumbling that went along with it, rowing had, at one time, been Beth's favorite sport. She'd even thought about getting serious about it, maybe get a scholarship to one of the more prominent rowing schools. But a scholarship could've taken her away from Nick, and she decided to attend school wherever he ended up.

She ordered a single scull from the kid managing the rental stand, strapped on the required life jacket. At the edge of the water, she stepped into the boat, rocked it a little, a bit unsteady on her feet. Maybe she was still tipsy from the beers, but she could manage. She needed to get out on that water and clear her head, feel the burn of the muscles in her arms, the sting in her lungs, and the water's spray on her legs. She was a bit rusty, sure—it had been a least ten years since she'd rowed a scull—but knew the motions would all come back to her. With the oars braced, she pushed off and began to navigate toward deeper waters.

From the bank, she saw Nick momentarily pause after completing a pass, to watch his wife go out alone. He was probably worried about her, given the conversation he'd overheard, but she would be fine. Right now, she just needed to row. *Row, row, row your boat.*

Out in deep water, the muscle memory in her arms and legs took over, just as she'd expected. As her legs pushed out, she pulled the oars against the water, then buckled her knees as the oars came around for another pass. She breathed in, breathed out, getting into the rhythm. Could almost hear the former shouts of the coxswain demanding she go faster. *Row, row, row.*

The more Beth rowed, the better she felt. The farther she got away from the shore—and those rumors—the clearer her head seemed. She'd like to say she was sorry for her outburst, but she wasn't. Except for the not-cheating part, she'd meant what she'd said—she truly believed Nick couldn't or wouldn't ever hurt another human being. In sixteen years of marriage, he'd never so much as raised a finger to her or one of the kids. He just didn't have a mean bone in him. Beth had always known him as more of the strong, silent type that commanded action with his words.

Yet, sometimes Beth sensed that there was another side to Nick. She often felt that he was concealing something from her, something even greater than the truth about his encounter with Missy. She didn't know what, but about once every month she'd find him sitting in a dark room alone, staring absently out the window, or walk in on him in his office at a moment when his face was nearly unrecognizable. Oftentimes, he would be making a fist and slowly pounding it into the palm of his other hand while grinding his teeth—as if he was holding in something dark and terrible.

But what? What could it possibly be? And why hold it back from her?

She understood why he'd never been able to come clean to her about sleeping with Missy. The weeks and months after Missy had confronted them at the homecoming dance, Beth had become a wreck, and Nick had, on more than one occasion, mentioned and questioned her fragileness. Perhaps he'd suspected she knew, or had heard, something about that night on the lake, or even suspected beforehand that something was going on between them. Certainly, the way Missy had stalked him all those months hadn't helped. But after homecoming, there wasn't anything Nick could do or say to console her. So, she understood his hesitancy to speak of anything Missy Ferguson. Given Beth's past breakdown, he would never, ever risk telling her the truth.

But, why not tell her what else was bothering him?

Unless...it also had to do with Missy Ferguson?

She kept rowing, letting the spray of the water splash over her legs, the wind whistle down the back of her neck. *Row, row, row.* It felt so good, the strain on her muscles, the burn in her legs, she wondered why she'd ever stopped spending so much time on the water. She thought back to the many times she'd rowed a scull or boat on this lake, out to the cabins, even into the marshes beyond—although the rules forbid it.

Out into the marsh, where the lake became strangled with cattails and grasses of various kinds, where beavers and otters swam. The preserve. No one was to cross over into the preserve. That area was dedicated to local wildlife and plants, part of

Michigan's rich heritage. She imagined herself back out in the marsh at dark, hearing those oars course the water, the night brightened only by the pale moon. Just a spotlight on the lake with an extended reflection where she would see the occasional ripple. She imagined the last time she'd rowed out to that sacred place, farther than she'd ever rowed before. She hadn't been thinking clearly that night, her mind upset and entangled by the latest events. The oars had stretched, her muscles had torn, and she'd become stuck. She'd been forced to stop and cried, broke down out there under a dark Michigan sky that opened and poured tears of its own, a late-autumn night when the temperature was approaching freezing. Back when...

She took a breath, squinted, could barely see the far bank where the reunion continued. An image, distant against the late-day sunlight, seemed to be beckoning her. Nick in a row boat? Then a second image, just a flash, of Nick standing on a similar bank of a sandy shore with something heavy draped across his arms.

What the hell?

Nick carrying a body up a hill.

Beth stopped rowing. Breaths, heavy like iron, stabbed in and out of her lungs like knives. Muscles, burning like the homecoming bonfire, melted under the weight. She placed her hands on the edges of the scull, tried to contemplate what she was imagining, and why?

She glanced up, shook her head slightly to erase the visions that had distracted her from her row. The air was cool and clean, helping to clear her thoughts. Beth looked around her and realized no banks of land now surrounded her—she'd rowed out much farther than she'd thought, far beyond the single scull boundaries. In the distance, she saw another image of Nick, this time motioning frantically with both arms, several people standing behind him. *What?*

She couldn't understand why he appeared so panicked.

Until she turned to see a longboat with eight rowers all coming directly toward her. Facing backward with no coxswain to guide their path, they didn't see her as she glided into the middle of the bigger lake. The force of their crash took their boat up and over Beth's tiny scull, and the next thing Beth McCallum knew, she was in the water.

9

I, Beth, Take Thee, Nick

The day Beth McCallum married Nick Storvik was the happiest of her life. For eight long years, she'd dreamed of this day, visualizing everything from the location, to the dress, to the cake. Nick let his bride decide upon everything— his only request being that she keep the guest size manageable, no more than one hundred people. Beth thought it was adorable that a man who could play football in front of thousands had a difficult time speaking and engaging with large crowds when he was the focus of attention.

For the location, Nick's mom, Susie, had suggested the same place she and Nick's father had gotten married, the Inn at Stonecliffe on Mackinac Island. The summer there was gorgeous, she promised, and after a quick trip one long weekend, Beth and Nick had discovered she was right. The place was beautiful, with an expansive outdoor lawn and venue next to Lake Superior. As soon as they learned the Inn was also able to provide the mandatory full bar and plenty of room for dining and dancing, they booked it for their special day—June 22, 2002.

Nick's and Beth's parents had long since resolved to becoming in-laws and, unlike so many families, got along famously. There was no infighting among them, no arguments over traditions or guest lists, no hurt feelings if Beth consulted one mother on colors or flowers or the menu selection and not the other. In alone times, Beth's parents had fretted over how much money the ceremony would cost them, but Nick's parents had graciously offered to pay for the rehearsal dinner and the reception, and that took a load off their minds. Nick's parents had also later advanced the newlyweds a down payment to purchase their first house as a wedding present, and Beth's parents, instead of taking offense, thanked them profusely for their generosity.

How many families could say their extended family got along so famously?

Not many, Beth knew.

In all the wedding planning, the dress had proved to be Beth's biggest obstacle, a dilemma between an antique ivory lace dress worn by Beth's maternal great-grandmother when she married in 1919, or a contemporary designer A-line gown with beaded embroidery and English net that Beth had fallen in love with after visiting a bridal store in Ann Arbor. Though her mother was disappointed that her only daughter didn't choose the family option, she acquiesced to Beth's wishes. It was Beth's dream day, after all, and she would only be doing this once.

After much debate, the colors Beth settled upon for her big day were royal purple and light gray. The bridesmaids wore matching satin A-lines of purple and the groomsmen gray tuxedos with purple bow ties. The day she and Nick married on that lawn next to the lake was a glorious June day—mid seventies with a light breeze and a few puffy white clouds in the sky, and the daylight hours were at their longest so the party could continue long into the night. Nick's niece and nephew, with their platinum blond hair and dimpled chins, made their wedding debut as flower girl and ring bearer, and brought smiles and laughter to the guests. But it was Nick's and Beth's vows that the guests said they remembered most, written personally by the couple.

I, Beth, take you, Nick, to be my husband. I promise to love you with all my heart and soul, to be the love in lover, the care in caretaker. I promise to create and support a family with you, in a household filled with laughter, patience, understanding, and love. I vow not just to grow old together, but to grow together. I love all that I know about you now, and I will love all there is to learn about you in the future. I promise to always be your biggest fan, as well as your partner in crime. I will love you faithfully, not just through the easy times, but through the most difficult of times. Whatever may come, I will always be there. As I have given you my hand, so I give you my life—to keep, to cherish, to protect. I trust you in all that you do now, and all that you decide for us in the future. I, Beth, am your wife.

The guests melted in a puddle of tears. There, on that lakefront, they watched a young couple exchange vows after being together eight years, since they were just fourteen and fifteen years old. It made the older in the crowd nostalgic for days gone by, when people formed relationships at a young age and took commitments seriously, and it made the younger hopeful, that one day they, too, could find such an unbreakable bond. Together, Nick and Beth had survived puberty, high school pressures, and college temptations. They had overcome lures and enticements, offers of other dates and unions, and, of course, *her.*

They stood on that lawn, the lake stretching out and glistening in front of them, telling of their future full of promise, miles of smooth sailing with few waves. They held hands, spoke their vows, expressed their love, promised to be together forever.

And now, only death could part them.

10

She Has Risen

A fter a quick check up at the local emergency room, the doctor pronounced Beth good and released her. He told Nick to watch Beth for any signs of confusion or headaches that suddenly came on, as she may have received a mild concussion from the impact of the boat capsizing, or the blunt of the oar knocking her on the head. Beth felt like an idiot and apologized repeatedly to both Nick and the doctor. She just wanted to get out of the hospital, go home, and return to her normal life.

Nick put his arm around her, lead her out of the ER, and helped her into the car. Dark now, he turned car's lights on and pulled from the parking lot. Although he stayed quiet, Beth knew the questions would soon be forthcoming, the same inevitable inquiries she was asking herself: What the hell had she been thinking, rowing out past the break line like that, into the path of the bigger sculls and sailboats? What had possessed her, other than the bulk of sunshine and water spray upon her face?

You, Nick. It was you. Standing on the side of a lake.

You, carrying a dead body.

Of course, she couldn't tell him that. He'd think she was losing it. No, she would simply blame the alcohol—it was never a good idea to drink in the sun. Still, she couldn't discount those images that had consumed her thoughts, taken over her consciousness.

Flashbacks to reality? Or just anxiety because of the rumors and the discovery of Missy Ferguson? Beth had long been prone to anxiety attacks, and it was just like her to fear and imagine the most awful of things during those bouts. Sometimes, especially first thing in the morning when waking from a particularly vivid dream, her heart would pound and the worst possible things she could envision raced through her thoughts—her children abducted and murdered, Nick killed in a car accident, a shooting at one of the schools. Sometimes, she would work herself into such a frenzy rolling through the possibilities that she'd find herself crying uncontrollably and hyperventilating. She didn't know why she thought about such terrible things. Fear, she supposed. The doctor told her it was quite natural, for our deepest fears often surfaced when our subconscious was at its most relaxed, but Beth hated such mornings. The doctor had taught her several meditation techniques she could use when such anxiety attacks occurred.

After they reached the hotel and entered the suite, Beth kicked off her shoes and lay down on the bed, then implemented one of those techniques. In fifteen minutes, she was breathing easier. Nick sat beside her, stroking her hair. "Feeling any better?" he asked.

"Some, yes. I feel like such an idiot."

Even with her eyes closed, she could sense Nick examining her. "I take it the women from our class continued to talk and upset you. Was it something specific that set you off? You were rowing those oars like your life depended on it."

Row, row. Yes, row. Row away, fast, and hard.

But why? Why had she felt that way?

She rolled to her side, snuggled close to herself. She didn't want to talk about it. Nick brought the covers up and over her. Those idiot women and all their talk and innuendo had planted terrible thoughts in her mind. How ridiculous of her to think such thoughts. Nick carrying a body. Her husband couldn't hurt anyone, not ever. Thank goodness Beth didn't have to face them anymore. Tomorrow they would go home and all would return to normal.

Nick kissed her cheek and cracked open a window to let in some fresh air. He left her alone in the bedroom of their suite, leaving the door ajar, and soon, Beth drifted into a soft sleep.

Until a soft knock and voices outside the bedroom woke her sometime later.

"I'm sorry to bother you again, but we need to talk."

Who was that? She recognized that voice. *No, it can't be.*

"Now?" Nick asked.

"I'm afraid so."

Jake Waters. Damn. Beth opened her eyes.

"Beth's asleep in the other room. I don't want to wake her," Nick said.

"No need. It's you I need to talk to."

She heard her husband sigh. "Fine, come in." He wasn't happy.

She sensed a rustling, Nick near the bedroom checking on her before he closed the door a little more. Beth really had to focus to hear their voices.

"Okay, what's this about? Or do I really have to ask?" Nick asked.

"No, you don't." A hefty sigh. She could almost see Jake putting his hands on his hips. "We learned today that the medical examiner was able to confirm that Missy was pregnant when she was killed. They found fetal bones. Small, but enough to get DNA. That means she was into her second trimester, about five months along."

Beneath the covers, Beth gasped.

Silence from Nick. "What's that got to do with me?" he asked. His voice was strange, tense.

"I need you to submit a DNA swab to rule you out as the father. If you never had sex with her as you claim, then you obviously have nothing to be concerned about. But, Nick, if you did, and you refuse to submit your DNA or try to hide your relationship with her and we find out later that this child is yours, that's not going to look good. That's probable cause."

Beth's stomach tumbled. The prior anxiety of the day returned with a vengeance. Fetal bones. They'd found proof. The worst news possible. But five months, that was too long, wasn't it? She counted. Early June to late October, when Missy had dropped out of school, wasn't quite five months. But it was close. Maybe too close. *Damn.*

Beth thought she was going to be sick. She closed her eyes.

Oh, Nick, why? Why did you ever have to...?

"Jake, I can't give you my DNA. No attorney would advise me to do that."

"Even to exonerate you? Why not? You told me you didn't have sex with her."

Footsteps, heavy, across the floor. More sighing. Nick exasperated. Beth could imagine him in the next room, hands on hips, biting his lower lip, pacing around like a caged tiger.

"I can get a court order if I need to, Nick," Jake said. "I don't want to do that."

Jake's voice raised, but it was still a whisper of itself. "Based on what? Rumors?"

"I might have some other evidence that would convince a judge, including Missy's diary documenting your encounter and you later shunning her, along with the pregnancy test results from the clinic. There was also some other evidence discovered at the burial site. I'm not saying it leads directly to you, but I'm not saying it doesn't either. You want to take that chance?"

Beth held her breath, felt her brow furrow. *Evidence? What kind of evidence? Showing he was at the scene?* That image of him standing on the lakefront resurfaced, holding a woman's body in his arms.

Oh, Nick, no.

"Jesus, Jake, what are trying to do to me here?" Nick asked. His previous whisper was growing into a raspy murmur. "Do you know what Beth would do if she found out I lied about sleeping with Missy Ferguson? I could lose everything. My wife, my kids. Jake, please..."

"And did you?" Jake asked.

"What?"

"Did you lie?"

Silence, then back to a whisper. A single curse. "Shit." She heard him fall into the couch, sigh. She could imagine him running his hands through his hair, across his face.

Beth felt a tear run down her cheek. She sat up, alarmed. He was going to confess. He was going to tell Jake the truth about sleeping with Missy Ferguson. She had to do something, and quick. "Nick?" she called out.

A moment later, he came to the bedroom door. "Yes? You okay?"

"I thought I heard voices," she said, pretending to still be sleepy. "Is someone else here?"

He glanced over his shoulder. "Yes, just a guest asking about the Wi-Fi. I'll see them out. Sorry for waking you." He shut the door. Beth could now only perceive the mumble of their conversation, but within five minutes, she heard Jake's footsteps descend the stairs outside. Sliding to the side of the bed, she peeked through a sliver of the curtain, and observed Jake as he walked across the parking lot. Outside the door to his truck, he stopped and took out his cell phone, made a call. Beth really wished she could hear what he was saying into that phone.

It was quite clear now that Jake suspected Nick in the murder of Missy Ferguson. But why, other than the old rumors? What other evidence was Jake referring to?

Nick opened the door, caught Beth glancing out the window. Neither said a word, just stared at each other for what seemed to be an eternity. "Can we go home now?" she asked. "I really just want to go home."

"No problem. I've already packed our things."

11

Relentless

After their time together, Missy Ferguson wouldn't leave Nick alone. Persistent in her original pursuit of him, she now relentlessly stalked him on other matters—most notably her claim to be pregnant. First, she told him of her missed period, then a second. Next, she brought him the pregnancy test, then the clinical results. Panicked, and with Beth clinging to him like a scared kitten, Nick brushed off all of Missy's further attempts to speak with him in person, refusing her phone calls and avoiding her at all costs. At the lake and out in public, he always made certain to surround himself with a posse of friends. In his mind, he thought she would just eventually tire of the matter and go away, but his act of denial and feigned ignorance backfired. By the time school started, she'd become openly aggressive in her pursuit. She attended his football practices and stood on the sidelines. She cornered him in the halls and classrooms at school. She even once came to his house and spoke with his parents when he wasn't present, explained to them how she and Nick had been dating.

And Nick had grown horrified. Told her to back off. Leave him alone. Get an abortion. Which only served to ignite her fury even more.

She pushed back. Started shoving her way into his midst even when surrounded by friends. Asked what they were going to do. Told him she wanted to keep the baby. Ears began to hear and lips proceeded to talk. It wasn't long until he couldn't breathe anymore. She was slowly suffocating him, holding a noose around his neck, and continuously pulling it a little tighter.

Finally, he'd succumbed and met her in private. He attempted to placate her, told her everything would be fine, even lied and said he cared deeply about her and the baby. But Missy Ferguson wasn't stupid. She tested his words by demanding he leave Beth and marry her, and Nick had erupted.

Never, never, never.

Once she knew he had no intention of getting involved or helping her out, the claws had come out. She'd grown tired of Nick ignoring her. She taped condoms to his locker along with a nasty note. She mailed his parents *Congratulations on Your New Baby* cards. She left a dead rabbit on Nick's porch.

And all the while, Nick tried desperately to shield Beth from the truth. Since she'd given herself to him on the Fourth of July, just as planned, he'd felt nothing but shame and remorse for sleeping with Missy a month earlier. He didn't know if it was just his guilt wreaking havoc with him, or if Beth had heard rumors that made her doubtful of his devotion, but ever since his time with Missy in that cabin, he swore Beth had looked at and treated him differently. There seemed to be a trace of sadness and disappointment highlighting her eyes, and although she'd never questioned his love before, she now constantly asked for reassurance. "Are you sure?"

The public outing at homecoming had been purposeful, of course. He should've seen it coming. Missy's desperation and anger had grown to a near frenetic pace those last few weeks, and she no longer cared who she hurt. Looking back now, Nick wondered why he'd ever fallen for Missy's temptations, realizing how manipulative and calculating she was. All he'd had to do was show a little restraint and none of it would've happened. Not the public confrontation, not Beth's meltdown, and, ultimately, not Missy Ferguson's death.

It was all Nick's fault.

As he drove, Nick stared into the dark night, watching the headlights of the passing cars approach and fade. He looked over into the passenger side where Beth lay curled on the reclined seat, sleeping. He listened to her steady breathing, wondered what she would think of him if she knew the truth. He pondered whether she was even really sleeping, or like him, obsessing about Jake's visit. She'd seen Jake leave, knew Nick had lied about their evening visitor. The morning would bring questions.

Nick sighed, fearing he was going to have to come clean. He had often thought about telling Beth the truth about his night with Missy and pleading for forgiveness, but given how she'd reacted after Missy's public announcement of her pregnancy and insinuation that Nick was the father, he'd always been afraid it would push Beth over the edge. That's why neither of them could, or would, ever talk about it—*her*—with each other.

The course of events that had occurred over the month after that homecoming dance made for the most terrifying time in Nick's life. Beth had descended into a state like he had never seen—crying one minute and hyperventilating the next, followed by a week of a near catatonic reaction. She would stare at the walls for hours, unblinking, or take off walking in a trance. She wanted nothing to do with anyone, especially Nick.

No words could comfort her, no touch could heal her, no amount of reason could reach her. Nick had believed that this would be the end of their relationship, that he had lost her.

Beth's parents had grown so concerned they'd taken her to see a psychiatrist. Nick was not supposed to know, but one night they had come to him and asked to know what had set their daughter off down such a dark road. After informing his own parents, he repeated the story, telling them of Missy's allegation against him and how Beth had responded—by attacking her. He denied the allegation was true, of course. Told them Missy was obsessed with him and was crazy, just like he informed everyone else. And they believed him.

The psychiatrist diagnosed Beth's behavior as post-traumatic stress disorder, but Nick just couldn't imagine how that single event at homecoming had caused Beth such a reaction. Yes, he knew Beth carried a mark of vulnerability, like a fragile crack etched upon her skin that, once pierced, created a cut so wide it exposed muscle and bone. It was due to that fierce loyalty she practiced and demanded, that protection of friends and family taken to near obsession. Still, Nick didn't think that one incident had been the sole cause of Beth's breakdown. He'd often wondered if there wasn't another encounter between Missy and her that he didn't know about, and although he'd asked, she never wanted to talk about it—or rather, *her*.

For twenty-two years, Nick had hoped neither Beth, nor anyone else, would ever discover the truth about him and Missy Ferguson. No one else had seen them that night, and he hadn't told anyone about their encounter, not even his friends, so he'd always thought it would be his word against hers, and no one could prove it any differently. And with her dead, it seemed foolproof, safely tucked in the past where it belonged.

Until tonight's disclosure by Jake Waters.

About a baby. About fetal bones. Bones forensic experts could use to extract and identify DNA. His DNA. Then Beth, and his parents, and all the world would know the truth of what he'd done. He'd slept with Missy Ferguson. He'd lied for two decades. And possibly, just possibly, they'd think he'd killed her too.

And there would be no escape from the wrath that would follow such a revelation.

He would lose his marriage. He would lose his kids. Worse, he would become a suspect in Missy's Ferguson's death. Everything he'd created and built would come crashing down because of one stupid night and a terrible decision. And Beth, she might take another deep dive into that depressive, catatonic state of before, and he couldn't stand the thought of it, Beth going back down that dark rabbit hole.

Nick had to do something. He had to make sure the truth never came to light. Not about his encounter with Missy, not about the baby, and certainly not about that night Missy had called him days after homecoming. When she'd begged him to meet her back out at the cabin—and he'd found her dead.

12

Home

The drive back to Ohio was uncomfortable and mostly silent. Beth's headache, once minor, had blossomed into a migraine and nothing she took seemed to relieve it. Nick questioned whether he should take her to a hospital, but she told him it wasn't necessary. She didn't believe it was because of the boating accident but due to seeing Jake Waters again. Nick seemed bothered by that, as if he were responsible for her feeling lousy.

In a way, he was.

As he'd driven and she pretended to sleep, she often peeked through one eye at her husband, watching the headlights of the passing vehicles light up the interior of the car—and Nick's face—before encompassing them in darkness again. In those brief shots of illumination, the deep lines of worry carved near his eyes and across his forehead made him appear more like the menacing man in that image she'd had at the lake and less like her husband. And she couldn't help but wonder...

Was it possible Nick could've killed Missy Ferguson?

She tried to think back to that time when Missy simply no longer showed up for school. After a week, her parents had filed a missing person report, but the authorities never took the girl's disappearance seriously once they'd learned of the terrible argument she'd had with her parents after informing them about her pregnancy, and, her father's admission he'd told her she was no longer welcome in his house. Once that hit the news, everyone believed she'd run away, either to have an abortion or to deliver the child elsewhere and never return.

For the last twenty-two years, Beth's greatest fear had been that one day, Missy would show up on their doorstep with Nick's son or daughter in tow. Now, she knew for certain that wouldn't happen, but the revelation of Missy's death had implanted in Beth a whole new fear—that her husband may have played a role in her murder.

What if Jake obtained his DNA and the tests came back positive? Could she live with Nick, knowing that he may have killed Missy? For years, she'd stood by his side and defended him, told others and herself that she and Nick had been together at the time of Missy's disappearance. Yet, no matter how much she tried to convince herself that was true, she knew there was a gigantic gap in her memory from that month, a time when her parents told her she'd gone to a very dark place and they'd been afraid of losing her forever.

She curled up in the seat and wrapped her arms over her head, trying to force it all away.

It wasn't until they arrived home near four a.m. and she took a long bath that her headache began to go away. While encased in bubbles, she reassured herself that all would now return to normal.

And for a time, it did. After going downstairs to find Nick's parents, the kids' sitters for the long weekend, in the sunroom reading the morning paper and the kids sitting around the kitchen table spooning cereal into their mouths and giving each other a hard time, all sense of normalcy returned. Nick came downstairs and drank from the milk carton, and his mother scolded him. Jacob attempted to catch pieces of toast in his mouth that Will threw from the opposite side of the table. Anna rolled the cereal around the bowl so she could avoid eating any of the green-colored circles. To Beth's great relief, it felt just like any other family morning.

She even relished the gigantic pile of dirty dishes in the sink. At times like these, during moments of anxiety, she preferred to wash the dishes manually, finding the act of scrubbing and cleaning therapeutic. And true to point, the more she scoured, the more her headache dissipated. Despite the noise and squabbling between the kids, Beth found it comforting compared to Jake Waters and her classmates with their constantly yapping mouths and speculating voices. She knew the more she could keep herself busy with laundry and cooking and running the kids to various practices and lessons, the more she could put the dreadful weekend, and thoughts of *her*, in the past, where she belonged.

She nearly made it a full day, until dinner.

After the kids had eaten and excused themselves to the next room to play video games, the adults settled in for dessert and coffee. It was Nick's mother, Susie, who started the conversation. "I know we really haven't had a chance to talk today, but we were surprised to hear you come in last night. We weren't expecting you until the day after tomorrow. What happened? Did everything go okay at the reunion?"

"My fault," Beth said, quickly intercepting Nick before he spoke. "I missed the kids."

Susie rolled her eyes. "Goodness gracious, Beth. You must get away occasionally. It's important for you two to have time to yourselves, believe me. Otherwise, you'll wake up one day and look to the other side of the bed and realize you don't even know each other anymore."

Beth sipped her coffee and glanced at Nick, wondered if that was already true. *How well do I know my husband?*

"Wasn't it fun catching up with your old classmates?" Susie asked. "Seeing who they married and what became of them?"

Nick grunted. "Not all of them," he mumbled.

Beth shot him a look. Truly, she didn't want to broach the subject. They'd experienced a good day. Couldn't they just keep it that way? She hoped he got the message.

"At my last reunion, we danced until the wee hours of dawn," Susie said. "We had so much fun."

"Yep," Nick's father, Ben, responded. "Your mom and I can still cut a rug." He turned to his son while placing a fork full of lemon cake into his mouth. "You didn't have any fun? None?"

Nick set his cup down. "Unless you count getting interrogated by a former classmate who is now a detective for the local sheriff's office as fun, I'd have to say, I most definitely did not have fun."

Beth focused on her coffee. Message not received. *Why did he have to bring it up?*

His mother's former smile disappeared. "What? What on earth for?"

"You didn't hear before you left town?" Nick asked. He checked over his shoulder to make sure the kids were out of earshot of the dining room and kitchen. "Last month, a construction crew uncovered some bones on an old portion of the wildlife preserve. They identified the bones last week as belonging to Missy Ferguson. Remember her?"

Susie Storvik gasped. "That girl that was so obsessed with you? That was her?"

Beth's head began to thump again. She rubbed it absently.

"I thought she ran away," Ben said.

Nick raised an eyebrow. "Apparently not. In fact, they believe she was murdered."

Another sharp intake of breath from Susie. "But I don't understand. Why would they want to talk to you?"

Nick reddened. Beth could tell he didn't want to explain, so she spoke up. *Might as well get it on the table. They would find out from the newspapers soon enough anyway.*

"Because they discovered Missy was pregnant when she died, and the baby's father is their likely suspect. Because of the allegations Missy made in high school, they think the father could be Nick."

A lump went down Nick's throat. "They want me to submit my DNA."

The color drained from his father's face. "What? Why? You had nothing to do with that girl."

Nick shrugged. "I...we..." he said, motioning toward Beth, "explained that to the detective. We told him the last time either of us saw Missy, we were at the lake, together. But, I don't know. Last night, he told me he could get a court order for my DNA if necessary."

He went on to tell them about the entire conversation with Jake—the threat of using Missy's diary and the pregnancy test to force Nick to submit his DNA, the suggestion of other evidence he couldn't name but which might implicate Nick. In his summary, it was obvious Nick was explaining to Beth, as well as his parents, what he'd said, probably hoping to prevent a repeat of the story later. Beth took note that he excluded his slipped admittance to Jake that he'd lied about sleeping with Missy Ferguson, preferring instead to stay with the claim that he'd never touched her.

"Well, clearly this detective is bluffing about the evidence," his father said. "He's trying to trap you into admitting something you didn't do. As if you were at the scene and knew about this girl's murder." He huffed, disgusted that anybody could suspect his son of such a thing.

Susie looked horrified, clasping a hand to her breastbone. "Nick, honey, this is terrible. You need to get a lawyer right away," she whispered.

As his parents' inquiries continued, Beth began to feel herself withdraw. With every one of their questions, with Nick's shifting eyes and lying tongue, the pounding in her head grew in intensity and depth. She could feel herself cracking, splitting like an egg, ready to break.

She stood to clear the dishes. She had to keep active. The day had gone so well, and now she was sliding back into her previous state of anxiety and despair. She had to distance herself from this. She thought they'd be able to return home and forget about this dreadful weekend and the news of Missy Ferguson, but now she feared this woman was going to live among them forever. She'd risen from the grave and was now haunting them, following them home and invading their lives all over again.

It made her so angry, her inability to get rid of this woman. She scrubbed and polished the latest dishes until they were so clean that she could see her reflection. Still, Nick and his parents continued to talk about Missy in the next room, even though Nick damn well knew Beth didn't want to hear about *her*.

She pressed the rag so hard against the plate in her hand that it shattered.

Susie heard it and yelped. Nick quickly rose, joined her in the kitchen, and grabbed the pieces of china. He examined Beth's hands for cuts.

"I'm fine, I'm fine. It just slipped." The three of them gathered around her, concerned and smothering. The kids also ran in, asked if she was all right.

So many people. So much attention.

Damnit, couldn't they all just shut up?

"We're sorry, Beth. We should've known better," Susie said.

Beth dried her hands, threw down the dish rag, sent the kids away before turning back toward her husband and in-laws. "Yeah? Well, I for one am not sorry at all. Frankly, I'm glad Missy Ferguson is dead, and I would like her to stay that way."

13

Bad Dreams

B
eth once had a dream that she'd murdered someone. It wasn't one of those average dreams where you wake up and say to yourself, *that was strange*, or *why did I dream that of all things?* No, it was one of those rare lucid dreams where you felt plunged into a parallel universe, living a different life, and experiencing every moment. She'd had other similarly vivid dreams before, just none as terrifying.

Once, she dreamed a group of alien visitors surrounded her. After landing at what could only be a space port, the equivalent of a bus or train station on Earth, she met with several alien governors who informed her of a gift she held—that of time travel. The universe only granted a few this power, an ability that allowed her to travel back to previous centuries and eras and change the course of events. In front of her was a massive ornate iron globe with many moving arrows and items rotating around it. The aliens explained to her the globe was a model of the entire galaxy, imprinted with a universal time clock that represented all the hours, years, and locations in the solar systems. As a designated traveler, they needed her to assume a new mission—to save a planet lost centuries before—one which displayed the most fragile but brilliant eco-system the likes of which existed nowhere else in the entire universe. Once destroyed, they could no longer recover or recreate all the precious species lost, and unfortunately, a few rogue inhabitants on the planet of otherwise pacifist beings had accomplished exactly that.

They sent Beth to this planet back before its destruction, and to say the plant and animal life exceeded her wildest imagination would be like saying the Taj Mahal was a simple house. Of her own accord, she flew past a large triangular tent-like structure pitching high into the sky, only to sense a fabric of an unrecognizable texture, strong as steel yet as thin as a butterfly's wings. She flew over the valley below where flowers carpeted the hills, each of them giving off the strangest of odor and whose petals were a color she couldn't describe—violet laced with bluish green and nearly opaque. At the bottom of the valley was a moving body she could only call a river, yet the substance that filled it she could not possibly call water. The thickness was more like that of a salve or ointment, but the element teemed with life. Spotting the landscape were dwellings of a white bubbly stucco nature with oval windows, each occupied by small citizens that resembled more bear than human but walked upright. And she could sense their joviality and spirit, even while flying high above them.

After that dream, Beth had risen with an insistence to note every detail of this new magical world that she could remember. It seemed she had traveled there overnight, and had now suddenly returned to her alternative life. At breakfast, she'd rambled on to Nick about how we didn't yet know all the physical and relational properties of the world and she'd seen some of them in her travels, and oh my God, did he know other colors existed?

The twinkle in his eye had told her how amused he was at her excitement.

The murder dream had been like this—palpable, real—but absolutely anything but exciting. Because in this dream, instead of transporting her to another world, place, and time, it cast her into the same world, but as another being. A shell of her that resembled her, yet wasn't like her at all, one completely devoid of feeling. In this being, Beth could remember committing actions that should've left her horrified and outraged, but there was nothing, not a drop of sorrow or despair or empathy of any kind. It was as if a cold, hard rock had replaced the heart. And more than the physical act of murder she'd performed in this altered reality, it was this dark, empty void of emotion that frightened her more than anything.

Where was the soul that belonged in this shell of a human being?

In her dream, she met with a man who was her husband. Again, like Nick, but not Nick. Together, they got into an old car, a brand and model Chevrolet don't even make anymore, and drove the dark country lanes out to a long-abandoned sand and gravel plant. The place looked like it hadn't seen life outside a stray dog or raccoon in the last ten years, but many of the previously dug pits and equipment remained— rusted out frontloaders, dump trucks, and Bobcats. The conveyer belts that had once carried material from truck to ground and vice versa hung at strange angles across the landscape, like the mechanical arms of a robot. It was as if the entire plant had shut down, the workers had abandoned their equipment, and management had simply locked the place up.

It was near one of these arms, toward the back of a large pyramid of sand now hardened by years of rain and freeze, that Nick stopped the car and told her to get out. Beth, ever obeying, slid from the passenger seat, walked to the trunk, and snapped on a set of gloves. Then, as if she did this every day, she opened the trunk and removed a woman. The woman, wriggling and desperate, looked up at her with wide, fearful eyes and moaned beneath the duct tape solidified across her mouth, but the actions and sounds only served to annoy Beth. So, Beth dropped her on the ground, kicked a boot full of dirt over her, and coldly told her to shut up.

As the woman cried and rolled around, trying to loosen the rope tied to her hands and feet, Beth began to carve away at the side of the hardened sand pile, creating a cave just wide enough to place a body in. Then, as if it made no difference to her whatsoever, she scooped up the young woman and stuffed her into the hole. The woman attempted to fight, to claw and kick and scream, but she was no match for Beth's determination. The woman had gotten in Beth's way—for what, Beth didn't know—and now, the woman had to die. Because that's what Beth—or rather, this woman who pretended to be Beth—did when others crossed her and messed with her friends.

And after she pushed this woman in, with a laugh that still made Beth's skin crawl to this day, she grabbed a long stick and poked at the higher, stickier sand until it began to sift downward over the woman as if she were on the underside of an hourglass. Then, Beth simply leaned against the back of the old car and watched until the hole filled in on itself and the muffled sounds of a desperate and pleading woman ceased to exist.

14

Could He?

Beth woke the next morning to find Nick rolled on his side staring intently at her. Surprised, she made a little startled sound before she realized it was him. He apologized and brushed a few loose strands of hair back from her face before wishing her a good morning. It was meant to be a caring gesture, but something about the way the tips of his fingers glided across her cheek gave her the chills. She pulled the covers over her shoulders, blamed her goosebumps on the open window.

The light smile that graced his lips faded. "You doing okay?"

"Yes," she mumbled, still half-asleep. "Just tired."

"Yesterday was a long day."

"Yes, as were the three days before. Some of the longest days of my life, I think. I hope starting today, we can all just return to normal."

"Yeah, that would be nice, wouldn't it?" He sighed. "Why do I feel like that's never going to happen again?"

Beth glanced at him, slightly alarmed. His shoulders were slumped and his eyes were bloodshot, and he looked every bit the man who hadn't slept for days. Normally so fresh and positive, this distress seemed unnatural on him, like a blanket in the middle of summer draped over him for warmth. The events of the last few days were weighing on him.

He started to caress her face again, but she sat up, and swung her legs to the floor. She walked over to the vanity to check the dark circles beneath her eyes. "Are your parents still here?" she asked.

"No, they left early this morning. Couple of hours ago."

The vibe that emanated from the bed disturbed her. She glanced at him through the mirror before her, felt a ripple of concern race across her brow. Nick sat, hunched over, staring at his hands as he wrung them together. What was happening to her husband? He was supposed to be her strength, her rock. Right now, he looked like a man embattled.

"Beth? Do you still love me?"

She picked up a brush and ran it through her hair as if the question didn't disturb her. "Of course, I still love you. Why would you ask such a thing?"

He looked at his lap, gripped his hands around the gathered sheets. "I don't know. Because of all the speculation. I fear sometimes, wonder if you believe I've done things...things that wouldn't make you proud of me."

She put the brush down. Her heart erupted, pounding hard against her chest.

So, was this it? Was he about to confess? And to what exactly? Sleeping with Missy? Or something far worse? What if he told her he had killed Missy Ferguson? What if he confessed to her that her visions were true, that he'd carried a body, Missy's body, up the hill to the preserve and buried her there? How would she respond?

She wasn't ready to have this conversation.

"I should wake the kids," she said. After giving him a quick kiss on the cheek, she wrapped a silk robe around her and left the room. As routine, she knocked lightly on each of the kids' doors, poked her head in to issue a "good morning." Today was Tuesday and a school day, so they all needed to be out of the house by seven thirty. She went downstairs to start the coffee and make breakfast.

She'd already taken the day off from work, originally thinking they wouldn't return from Michigan until today, and had no plans to make changes. With Nick's parents already gone, she'd use the day to do laundry and clean, put everything back in its proper place.

Forget last weekend ever happened. Forget Missy Ferguson ever happened.

That's what she really wanted. Just to forget. She wished Nick could forget too.

Anna was first to come downstairs, followed by Will, then Jacob. Upstairs, she heard Nick taking a shower. The kids ate cereal and toast and spoke little while Beth drank coffee and relished watching them eat. Just seeing the three of them together made everything else better.

She helped Will and Jacob get out and off to the bus in time, assisted Anna with her lunch and backpack. She still couldn't believe her youngest was in kindergarten already. This would be her last go-around with elementary school, and Beth wanted to hang on to these days as much as she could. She wondered what the hell she would do when they were all grown-up and moved away.

When Nick came downstairs, Beth was surprised to see him dressed in business attire, including a tie. "You going into the office?" she asked. "I thought you took the day off?"

He shrugged. "I might as well get a head start on the week. No reason to burn a vacation day if I don't have to." He removed the milk from the refrigerator, drank. Grabbed a slice of toast and a banana. Still, he didn't look at Beth. "You want me to drop Anna off at school?"

"No, I'll take her," Beth said. "I've got some errands to run anyway."

Nick leaned over to kiss his wife and daughter and headed out the door. A nervousness stemmed from him like Beth had never experienced before, couldn't help but feel empathy for him. Nick was always the calm, collected one in their relationship, Beth the train wreck. This new Nick wasn't the Nick she knew at all.

Even Anna picked up on the disturbance. "What's wrong with Daddy?"

Beth stroked her daughter's hair. "Just a lot on his mind, honey. He'll be fine."

Beth dropped Anna off at kindergarten, then headed to her favorite drive-through café for a double espresso and a croissant. With everyone out of the house, she decided to take a few minutes and enjoy the silence in the parking lot to eat her breakfast. Rarely was she alone, so anytime she got the chance to just sit and breathe was a good thing.

She thought again about Nick. How he seemed to be coming undone. First, a detective questions him, then he sees his wife take a header into the lake, then the detective returns. It hadn't been a good weekend. There existed no doubt how disturbed Nick was by Jake's latest visit, with his threats to force Nick to submit his DNA and hints at evidence left at the scene of Missy Ferguson's death. But if Nick hadn't been there, then why should he worry? Of course, Beth knew the answer. If he provided his DNA and it was a match, the whole world would know Nick had lied about his relationship with Missy Ferguson. And if he could lie about sleeping with Missy, then he could lie about other things as well. And even if he had nothing at all to do with her death, nobody would ever believe it.

Maybe not even Beth.

I fear sometimes, wonder if you believe I've done things...

Her heart palpitated. Sitting there in the SUV, she wondered if it was time for both to confess their sins. Let him know she knew about Missy and him, overhead all of Jake's questions the other night. He had to be frantic, wanting to talk with somebody about it, and together, they could work to overcome whatever came their way. Yet, she also had fears about revealing the truth to him, and about his reaction to her keeping her own secrets for so long. What would it do to them and their marriage, knowing both had lied to one another?

Lies. So many lies. His. Hers.

Her brow furrowed when she saw Nick's truck pass on the street in front of her. Nick had left more than an hour ago, and this wasn't the way to his office. His office was in Cincinnati, the one he visited once or twice a week for meetings instead of working from home. He'd stated firmly he was going into the office. So, now... what? More lies?

Beth started the SUV and pulled out from the parking lot and on to the street. She decided to follow him, but at a safe distance. Three miles in, he turned toward the turnoff to the next town, proceeded another twenty miles until he reached the city limits.

What possible reason would he have for coming here, to a place they frequented only for football or baseball games against the rival schools? He wound through the main downtown area, circled around the courthouse square, came to rest in the parking lot of a three-story brick building. Got out and went inside.

Beth frowned. She had to find out who kept offices in that building. She pulled out her phone, activated the search function, and typed in the building's address. Sorted through the array of companies that surfaced—a media company of some kind, a consulting firm, a nonprofit for children. And an attorney's office—specializing in criminal defense.

Beth closed her eyes, felt her heart do a deep dive. *Damn.* He was speaking with an attorney. Preparing his defense if Jake tried to come after him, most likely, or discussing options if they should arrest him. Either way, she didn't like it. She didn't want other people involved in their private matters.

She quickly drove home, spent the day pacing about the house and cleaning, trying to keep her mind busy. She wasn't sure what she would say to him when he came home—whether to once again, keep her knowledge to herself, or ask him why he didn't go to the office. But how could she without confessing to following him?

Another secret to add to the others.

She stripped all the beds in the house and kept busy with laundry. Doing the wash always helped her calm down when she felt an anxiety attack coming on. It felt good to be in the laundry room, smelling bleach and clean clothes, taking care of her family.

When Nick returned around four p.m., Beth was sitting with Anna at the kitchen island, the two of them eating a snack of apples and cheese. Flushed, Nick mumbled something about a busy day and headed directly upstairs to his office. He looked haggard, as if whatever news or advice he'd received wasn't the message he'd wanted to hear.

Beth left Anna happily coloring a picture with crayons and decided to head upstairs to check on him. As she took a basket of clean clothes up to the kids' bedrooms, she stopped outside his office door, heard him talking on the other side. Already ajar, she silently pushed the door open farther ever so slightly, just until a crack appeared and she could see in. Nick was facing his desk, standing with his back to the door, one hand on his hip and the other holding the cell phone to his ear.

"How? You can't do that without my permission."

He listened. Turned his face up toward the ceiling, made a fist. Angry.

"Beth? No. I'm not going to tell her. It will only upset her. She damn near drowned two days ago. I'm not going to..." More listening. "Fine, you do that."

Beth felt her forehead crease, the skin across her cheeks and lips tighten. *Not tell me what?* He'd always been protective of her mind-set, ever since...that month.

"I'm just telling you. Regardless of the results, it won't prove anything."

After ending the call, he slumped forward and rubbed his face. Heaved a sigh that sounded like it came from the bottom of his lungs. Tired. Stressed. Concerned. Over something—but what? Who'd been on the phone? An attorney? Or Jake Waters?

Beth didn't like the claustrophobia that crept over her and settled in her pores, like the fog that tiptoed over the lake until you couldn't see two inches in front of your own face.

When he started to turn, she quickly disappeared down the hall and got busy in Will's bedroom, putting away folded socks and T-shirts. From the corner of her eye a few seconds later, she saw Nick's head pop out into the hall and look around. Seeing no one, her husband closed the door, followed only by the solid click of the lock.

15

I, Nick, Take Thee Beth

Nick stood nervously at the alter awaiting his bride's arrival. Why he was nervous, he had no idea. He'd always known he would marry Beth, never had a single doubt about her love for him. She'd stood by him when the principal had briefly expelled him from school for playing a prank, cared for him when he'd broken two of his fingers on his left hand, gave one of his friends a tongue-lashing when he'd repeatedly tempted Nick to try drugs. She was there through thick and thin, good times and bad. But privately, he wondered—would she still be walking down the aisle toward him today if she truly had any idea about what Nick was capable of? For six years he had kept his dark secret about Missy and the pregnancy to himself, fearing Beth would find out one day and leave him. Yet, here she was, parading down the stretch of lawn covered with a white runner sprinkled with rose petals, about to become his bride.

How did he ever get so lucky? What on earth did Beth McCallum see in him?

Her father beamed proudly while leading her down the aisle, their arms interlocked. Seated in the front, Beth's mother dabbed her eyes with a tissue, trying hard not to run her mascara. On the other side, his mother did the same. Their parents had always gotten along, friends from day one. He thought about how so many couples didn't like or get along with their in-laws. That wouldn't be their problem. Their friends, their family, loved them. Except for that one dark, singular moment, Nick and Beth had lived a charmed life.

So, he couldn't help but wonder, when would it all come crashing down?

They were playing "Here Comes the Bride" now. Beth's beautiful smile radiated beneath her veil, her eyes sparkling with joy. Nick's chest ached. He wanted to give it all to her. The beautiful house, the white picket fence, the perfect kids. They were already well on their way. They'd both recently graduated from the University of Dayton with degrees in business administration and marketing and had job offers on the table. Nick's parents had gifted them a down payment on a house, a cute bungalow Beth had fallen in love with instantly in an older but up-and-coming part of the city. He didn't care for it much, but it didn't matter. He wanted her to have whatever she wanted. Anything to make up for what he'd done. For the line he had crossed.

Why in the hell had he ever risked it? Giving himself to a girl who had no more love for him than a pet hamster? That night had nearly cost him everything. Until...

Would he go to jail for his deeds? Most certainly, he would. Which is why it had to remain a secret. Nobody could ever know. Including Beth. Especially Beth.

Here she was—his bride. His wife. His life. Since that first day he'd seen her in the halls of their high school until now, he'd known he was going to marry her, and now their day was here. He'd let her decide most of the wedding arrangements. The only things he'd given his input into had been the guest list, menu, and location. And, of course, the ring. That was all him. A two-karat double halo infinity ring in white and rose gold that had cost him a small fortune. But he didn't mind. He'd been saving for it since his senior year of high school.

The year after the bad year. The very bad year.

The minister was giving them direction now. Telling them about God's plan of marriage and structure for the family unit. A circle unbroken, a vow for them to take seriously. Unconditional love, for better or for worse, for richer or poorer, until death do them part. Followed by their own vows, written together, first Beth's, then his.

I, Nick, take you, Beth, to be my wife. I promise to love you with all my heart and soul, to be the love in lover, the provide in provider. I promise to create and support a family with you, in a household filled with laughter, patience, understanding, and love. I vow not just to grow old together, but to grow together. I love all that I know about you now, and I will love all there is to learn about you in the future. I promise to always be your biggest fan, as well as your partner in crime. I will love you faithfully, not just through the easy times, but through the most difficult of times. Whatever may come, I will always be there. I would gladly give my life for you, and promise to protect, honor, and shelter you and our children forever. I trust you in all that you do now, and all that you decide for our family in the future. I, Nick, am your husband.

There wasn't a dry eye in the crowd. How lucky he was. How so, so, very fortunate.

How close he'd come to screwing it all up forever.

He would stand firm and honor his vows. Protect his kids from any harm or rumor that could befall them. Honor his wife for the commitment and dedication she'd given him since day one. Shelter them all from ever knowing the truth about their father and Missy Ferguson.

He just prayed there would never come a day he would have to break that promise.

16

Secrets and Lies

N ick sat in the quiet of his office, trying, but failing, to get any work done. They'd been home for more than a week now, yet nothing felt near normal. Since Jake had called to inform him that he'd taken Nick's DNA from a beer bottle at the reunion, Nick had been pulling his hair out. He'd visited with attorneys to see if it was legal and, after learning that it was, started asking them questions about a possible arrest. He didn't know what else the police had—and he certainly hoped Jake was bluffing—but if they did, the attorney told him to expect an arrest. The pregnancy gave the police motive. If they discovered Nick was the father and found his DNA at the scene, then he was toast. Nick tried to explain to the attorney that even if he was the father, he wasn't Missy's killer, but even the attorney didn't look convinced. What made Nick think a jury would decide any differently?

He buried his head in his hands. Why had he ever convinced Beth to go to their reunion? For one of the few times in his life, Nick wanted to hang his head and cry.

He glanced at his phone, thinking about the call that could upend his life. He thought he now knew what Beth's anxiety attacks felt like—the walls in his office too close, the clothes on his skin too clingy, the breaths from his lungs too shallow. Since they'd returned, he'd been like a mouse caught in a trap, scurrying around looking for a way out of the mess he'd gotten himself into. And although he'd tried to maintain normalcy around the kids, they'd picked up on his uneasiness, kept asking him what was wrong.

He never wanted to do this, put this burden upon his kids. He'd vowed to protect, honor, and shelter Beth and their children forever. What would they think of their father when the police came to arrest him? When they took him away in handcuffs and placed him in the backseat of the police car? When every media outlet in the country displayed his face to the masses?

If he got that phone call, he wouldn't just break that promise, he would shatter it.

A loud buzz pervaded the room. But it wasn't the phone. It was the doorbell.

He went downstairs, glanced outside, stopped breathing. There was a truck parked in his driveway. A truck with Michigan plates. Jake's truck. *Damn, damn, damn.*

Was this it? Was he here to arrest him?

He glanced in the mirror, checked his face and hair, straightened his collar. Again, the doorbell. Jake was impatient. Nick took in a deep breath, steadied himself, opened the door. Saw his former classmate in jeans, a sport jacket, and cowboy boots, just like at the reunion. "Jake?"

"Hi, Nick. Sorry to drop in on you like this, but we need to talk."

Nick cocked his head. Glanced behind him to see if any officers or SWAT members were somewhere outside his house. "You couldn't call? Don't tell me you were just in the neighborhood. You know this is Ohio, right?"

"Yes. Can I come in?"

Nick swung the door wide, motioned him in. The smell of impending rain was heavy in the air, the sky turning dark. Jake's boots plodded against the hardwood floors. "Is Beth home?" he asked.

"No, but she will be soon, probably within the hour. Why?"

"Probably best...for now," Jake said, his voice as gruff as one of those cowboys in the old Westerns. "Someplace we can talk?"

Nick led him to his office upstairs, asked Jake if he wanted something to drink.

"I'm good," he said as he entered Nick's office. He walked slowly around the room, examining photos and knick-knacks, mostly sports memorabilia and photographs of Beth and the kids. He didn't sit so Nick didn't either. No reason to get comfortable and invite him to stay any longer than necessary.

"Work from home, huh?"

"Most of the time," Nick said. "So, what's this about, Jake? You get the DNA results?"

Jake picked up a photo of Nick and Beth, brushed off a light film of dust. "Good picture of you two." He set it back down. "Yes, I did get the results. And congratulations are in order."

Nick closed his eyes. *Here it comes. The doom.*

"You're not the father, Nick."

Nick's eyes flew open. He tipped his ear, sure he hadn't heard Jake's words correctly. He asked him to repeat it.

"You're not the father. Your DNA wasn't a match."

A rush of pulsing blood and air nearly sent Nick to the floor. He bent over, placed his hands on his knees, took several deep breaths. Said a string of prayers, thanks, and pleas for forgiveness to the God he too often ignored. He glanced up to see Jake with a wry grin.

"I take it by your reaction there was a chance it could've gone the other way, huh?"

There was no use denying the truth now. Nick's reaction had overridden everything he'd ever denied. Nick nodded. He stumbled to his office chair, collapsed more than sat in it. Wiped an unexpected tear from his eye.

Jake lowered himself into one of the matching chairs that rested on each side of a bookshelf. "Well, I hate to burst your bubble, but I should tell you that just because the DNA didn't come back as a match doesn't mean you're totally off the hook. You still had motive if you had reason to believe that the baby was yours."

Jake issued Nick a glare that said he continued to see him as suspect and was determined to find Missy's killer. "Tell me, why did you lie about it, your relationship with Missy?"

Nick took another deep breath, tried to calm the pounding heart in his chest. He needed to come clean with Jake. "Look, I slept with her, I did, but just once. One time, that was it. It was a terrible mistake. I lied to protect Beth. She doesn't know. For all these years, even with the rumors, she's stood by my side, kept believing me when I told her nothing happened. And I had to. I had to keep lying. When Missy confronted me publicly, after homecoming that year? Beth didn't take it well. Just the allegation alone caused her to have a breakdown. She went to a dark place, I mean, really dark."

"Did you two break up?"

"No, not exactly. Just, Beth wasn't herself for many weeks afterward."

Jake frowned. "In what way?"

"In every way." Nick stared at her picture on his desk. Sometimes, just seeing her glowing smile caused him great guilt. "She withdrew into herself. Didn't talk, didn't blink, didn't sleep. She was almost catatonic. Other days, she'd cry and wail for hours. Her parents finally took her to see a psychiatrist. They were extremely worried." Nick wrung his hands. "He diagnosed her with PTSD, for heaven's sake. Just over Missy's allegations. So, you see why I had to lie."

"Post-traumatic stress disorder," Jake said. "Hmm." He took out a small notebook, made a notation. "This was when? End of October, early November that year?"

Nick nodded. "Yes. It was a bad time, for all of us."

Jake huffed. "Not as bad as it was for Missy Ferguson," he said. "I promise you that."

A wave of nausea ran over Nick. He wanted to throw up.

"So, protecting Beth, that was why you lied about Missy? No other reason? I got the feeling when we spoke at the reunion that you might know something else...something about how or why Missy disappeared. Maybe the last time you saw her wasn't at the lake with Beth?"

You mean like when I went out to the cabins to meet her and found her dead?

Nick bit his bottom lip. No way in hell he could offer that bit of information. "No. It was just Beth. I wanted to protect Beth."

Jake nodded. He shifted in his chair, once again picked up a framed photograph, this one of Beth in front of a waterfall. "Nick?" he asked. "How well do you know your wife?"

Nick sat back, gave a half laugh. "What? We've been married for sixteen years, together for twenty-four. I think I know my wife pretty well, Jake. Thanks for asking."

He continued. "She's fragile. She breaks easily. I think it's because of this fierce loyalty she gives and demands. Ever since her real dad left her and her mom, she fears people leaving. Do you know—I'm the only man she's ever slept with? She's given her entire life to me."

Nick paused, thinking about that devotion, feeling the immense weight of its responsibility. "I betrayed her, and when I did, just the insinuation that I had betrayed her nearly killed her. You know what that did to me, Jake? To see her in that catatonic state because of me? That's why I lied. The only reason. Even more than worrying that my marriage might crumble if I told the truth, I feared what would happen to Beth."

His voice wavered with the last sentence, a swell of emotion getting to him.

Jake studied his lap, gave Nick a minute before speaking again. "You really don't think Beth knows the truth about you and Missy? I find it difficult to believe this single allegation would cause her to go into such a state of depression. You clearly keep secrets from her, what makes you think she hasn't done the same?"

Nick tightened his lips, annoyed at his former classmate's dissection of his marriage. Still, he couldn't deny he'd often questioned the same thing.

Jake flipped a couple of pages in his book. "Are you aware of an encounter between Beth and Missy that occurred at the local family clinic in early August of 1996? Missy's diary, in addition to discussing in detail your...time together, also tells of this run-in with Beth. It seems when Missy went in to get a pregnancy test, Beth was also there getting her birth control pills renewed. When Missy came running out of the doctor's office after learning of her condition, she ran into Beth. She details how she froze in front of Beth and how Beth boiled over. She wrote: '*I knew in that moment that Beth McCallum knew I'd slept with her boyfriend and was now pregnant with his baby.*'"

Nick felt a hard punch to his gut. Beth had never mentioned any such run-in. Though fear tainted with anger boiled in his veins, he tried to keep from showing any outward emotion.

"First, I wouldn't believe everything written in Missy Ferguson's diary," he said. "Second, even if Beth ran into her there and learned Missy was pregnant, at that point in time Beth would've had no reason to believe the baby was mine. Missy didn't confront me in front of Beth until much later, in early October, at homecoming."

Jake looked unconvinced. "Right, homecoming, when Beth reacted to the allegations by attacking Missy." He cocked his head. "Look, I know you said Beth was fragile, but I think we can both agree that Beth has another side—a jealous side, and when it flares, she grows angry and acts out."

Nick frowned. Thought of Jennifer Dansen's slashed tires, knew Jake was right. "Yes, sometimes. So?"

Jake removed some papers from the inside of his pocket, proceeded to unfold them. "You said Beth went to a dark place after that confrontation? Around late October, right? That was about the same time a park ranger found Beth in a row-boat deep in the marsh one night, wasn't it?"

Nick felt his brow furrow. He shot Jake a look. What the hell was he talking about?

He grabbed the papers from Jake's hands, put on his glasses to review them. It was a copy of a police report, dated October 26, 1996. Nick read over the details: female subject, age sixteen, matching Beth's description, found despondent. A park ranger had discovered her in the marsh north of the lake, outside the legal boating boundaries, confused and disoriented. The police expected drugs but tests came back negative. They called Beth's parents who later reported she was suffering from PTSD. The police took no further action and dropped trespassing charges.

Nick just stared. He didn't know what to make of it. Except...

Except he knew that date. It was the date he'd agreed to meet Missy at the cabin to talk, and he'd discovered her dead.

Oh my God. No. Oh my God.

He felt Jake's eyes upon him. "You were aware of this incident, weren't you? Her parents said she'd been experiencing episodes of sleepwalking, and she drove, unaware, out to the lake and took a boat out to the marsh. Beth claimed to wake up there and not have any memory of how or why she'd gone there. The park ranger said she was a real mess. Couldn't answer any of his questions."

A deep chill latched on to Nick's bones. Outside, the first crack of lightning flashed and the thunder roared, shaking the entire house. He felt the same inside. He wondered what time Beth would get home. Maybe the storm would delay her. He handed the papers back to Jake.

"What can you tell me about the incident?" Jake asked.

Nick shook his head. "Nothing. I wasn't even aware of it. Her parents told me about taking her to a psychiatrist, but nothing about this." He felt numb, outside his own body. "Maybe they thought it would make me feel worse than I already did—about her condition, I mean. Or maybe they didn't want to embarrass her. Beth doesn't even know that I'm aware about her time spent with the doctor. If she thought I knew about this..." He bit his bottom lip, frowned. "Damn. That encounter with Missy really messed with her head. I just don't understand it."

Jake checked his watch as another round of thunder boomed. "Well, I hate to say it, Nick, but I'm going to need to speak to Beth—question her about her knowledge of you and Missy Ferguson and about that night in the marsh. See, that's just about the time we believe Missy was murdered. She never returned to school the following week."

Nick's head began to spin. His world was crashing down. This wasn't happening. His wife? The mother of his kids? Suspected of murdering his old girlfriend?

Nick's mouth dropped open. He reeled. "Jake, come on. You can't possibly believe Beth had anything to do with Missy's death. Beth is five-foot-five. Missy was what, five-foot-nine or so? No way in hell Beth could drag her body through the marsh and up to dry land. Then what? Dig a grave and bury her? Come on."

He shook his head. He couldn't believe Jake could suspect his wife. "No, no, you can't talk to her about these things. This, all of this, has been so troubling for her already. Further questions could send her back down that rabbit hole. I can't take that chance."

"You're saying no?"

"Firm no. Not without a lawyer present and possibly a psychiatrist to monitor her condition."

Jake put his notebook away. "Well, I'll be in touch."

He started for the door when he paused and turned back around. "Oh, one other thing." He reached back in his pocket, removed what appeared to be a photograph, handed it to Nick. "Does this earring look familiar to you? You ever see Missy wear a pair like this?"

Nick took it, glanced at the photo of a red-and-white teardrop-shaped earring, now rusted. He made no sudden movements, no change of expression. Handed it back. "No, I don't think so."

"No?" Jake asked, doing a double take. "See, what's strange is, Missy was wearing earrings when she died. Two small gold hoops. They found those in her grave. But this one was just...random." He turned the photo back to Jake. "Red and white. Our school colors. You think that's just a coincidence?"

Nick shrugged. "Yeah, has to be."

But as soon as he saw Jake out, Nick collapsed onto the sofa and wrapped his hands around his head. *Oh, Beth. No. No. What the hell were you doing out in the marsh that rainy October night?*

17

Lost

B eth left the office at four p.m., having wrapped up for the day. She was anxious to arrive home and get dinner on the stove, pour herself a glass of wine, and check in and see how Nick was doing. All week long, he'd continued to be a ball of nerves, and Beth was beginning to worry. She panicked every time she heard a siren, held her breath when she saw a police car drive past their house. Would they come for him? Would they arrest him?

Was it possible Nick had killed Missy Ferguson?

Since that shielded phone call and trip to the attorney's office, Beth had struggled with that question. Every day now, she wrestled with more thoughts and recollections from that dreadful time, as well as the migraines that came with them. It seemed, like Missy, the memories no longer wanted to remain buried in some cold, dark grave. They tapped her on the shoulder. Woke her up in the middle of the night. Demanded her attention when all she wanted was to send them away.

And every day, she grew more afraid of what they would reveal to her. About Nick. About Missy. About herself.

She grabbed her purse and slung it over her shoulder, headed out of the office building. The sky was dark and gray, with low, heavy clouds that promised rain. She barely made it to the door of her SUV when the sky opened and it began to pour.

She stopped at the bank to deposit two checks, swung by the grocery for a roll of fresh-baked French bread, collected Anna from daycare. Ten minutes later, she drove down the street to their house and started to pull into the drive when she saw it—a truck with Michigan plates.

Beth hit the brakes, stared through the water streaming down her windshield. Stopped breathing. *No. It can't be. What the hell is he doing here?*

She thought of the reasons Jake Waters would drive all this way to speak with Nick, didn't like any of them. Nick questioned. Nick arrested. The DNA a match. She put the SUV in reverse and pulled out. Anna's voice from the backseat: "Where are we going, Mommy?"

"I just forgot something at the store, honey." Beth retraced the drive to the store, stopped at a red light. Let the engine idle. The windshield wipers clacked back and forth across the SUV's glass, desperately trying to keep up with the heavy rain thrashing down. Her head began to throb.

Beth closed her eyes. With every pass of the wipers, her heart raced a little faster. She could feel the anxiety swell within, like air in a balloon. Flashes of additional memories began to surface.

It had been a night just like this one when she'd gone out to the lake alone. It was a cool night in late October, the leaves thick upon the ground and the smell of impending rain heavy in the air. She couldn't remember driving to the lake, or why she'd been so intent on going there in the first place, but after she'd parked the car, she'd hiked over to the side of the lake where they rented boats, the booth long since closed, and took out one of the row-boats piled on the bank.

She'd rowed across the smooth, clear waters of the lake, out past the marina where owners had docked the bigger boats for the evening. She could hear the laps of the water pushing away from each side as she rowed, only interrupted by the occasional call of a night heron or hoot of an owl from the dense line of forest that set back twenty feet from the shoreline. The sky was dark, not a star or the moon lighting the night sky. The clouds had moved in and they intended to stay.

She was sixteen years old and out on the lake alone, just her and that boat and the sound of the water, *whoosh, whoosh*, when it all went black. A void of time, of memory, of purpose.

What had she been doing? Where had she gone?

One minute she'd been rowing across the smooth, clear waters of the lake, and the next she was deep in the marsh, where the lake grew clogged with cattails and grasses three feet high. And it was there in the marsh it began to pour rain, the kind of cold late-October rain that chilled your bones for days afterward with no chance of drying them out. She woke from her daze and attempted to get a handle on her surroundings. She glanced down at her jacket and shirt, splattered with an unknown substance, examined her jeans and tennis shoes, covered in mud and grime.

What the hell? Had she been outside the boat?

As the rain poured down, she cleaned herself off. Her mother would be angry at her for ruining her clothes.

She took hold of the oars, started to navigated away from the marsh. But which way was out? She couldn't see between the sheets of rain and the enveloping darkness. Anything, anyone, could be in front of or behind her. She began to panic, to call out.

But no answers came. Just the torrential downpour hitting the water with a sound like hail pounding upon a tin roof.

And then, lights. A park ranger with an industrial flashlight who'd heard what he said was the sound of Beth crying. Tying her boat to his and rowing her back to shore. Radioing ahead for the police. The red and blue lights flashing on the shoreline, awaiting her arrival. A woman officer putting a blanket over her shoulders, shining a small flashlight in her eyes. Asking her questions. Could Beth hear her? Did she know where she was? Could she tell the woman her name?

Beth could see a second officer standing behind the woman shaking his head. "Bad shape. She's in bad shape," he said. They motioned for the paramedics. Now more people were running over, examining her, and asking questions. But nothing that made sense. Their faces were just blurred images she couldn't discern. Their voices but words she couldn't distinguish.

And she was wet. So very wet.

What the hell had she been doing out there in the marsh?

She'd never told Nick of her accident, of going out to the lake in her depressive state and nearly dying. She begged her parents not to reveal it and they'd happily complied. No good could come from telling others, like teachers and academic counselors, about the event. What would they think of the episode, and Beth, after learning of her blackout? She was preparing to take the SAT and ACT, would be submitting applications to colleges soon. This wouldn't look good on her record. Thankfully, the police were sympathetic and dropped all charges against her upon learning of her condition: PTSD.

Her psychiatrist had later asked her what she remembered most about that night. Was it the drive out to the lake, the row across the water, or waking in the marsh? But it wasn't any of those things. What Beth remembered most about that night was the cold. The kind of cold that made your body stiffen, your face numb, and the air in your lungs freeze as if it were liquid. The kind of cold where you can't stop shaking and you lose all feelings in your extremities. They become disoriented, like the rest of you. So cold. So wet.

"Mommy?"

Beth gasped, blinked, slowly opened her eyes. Heard a loud honking behind her.

"The light is green," Anna said. "You can go now."

18

Could She?

After Jake's departure, Nick stayed in his office for two more hours, trying to decipher all Jake had told him. At once relieved over the news that he wasn't the father of Missy's baby, Nick was now distraught over the idea that his wife might've killed her, believing that he was. He'd long thought it odd how traumatized Beth had become after the homecoming incident, had long wondered if Beth and Missy had more of a history than he knew about, and now he suspected it was true. Had Beth heard rumors of Nick and Missy long before that homecoming dance? Had she suspected that he'd been unfaithful before encountering Missy at the clinic? How much did his wife know about him and Missy Ferguson?

Jake's question replayed in Nick's mind. *How well do you know your wife?*

He thought about that earring, Beth's earring, discovered in the grave of Missy Ferguson. The same one she wore on the sidelines of football and basketball games. If Jake Waters made that connection, there would be no hope for Beth. He'd take her in and interrogate her until he broke her. And it wouldn't take much.

What would happen to her? Would she remember and confess? Or would the shock of the allegations drive her back down to that deep, dark place? And what would Nick do when they hauled his wife off to jail or a mental ward?

Nick wanted to scream. Wanted to laugh off these thoughts that Beth could've possibly played a role in the death of Missy Ferguson. How could he think such a thing? His own wife? The mother of his kids? The woman he'd known for twenty-four years? There had to be a reasonable explanation that didn't involve murder.

Didn't there?

He chewed off his last remaining nail, heard Beth downstairs calling everyone for dinner. He had to play it cool for now, act as if nothing new had happened. Until he had some time to investigate the incident at the marsh, it wouldn't be wise to open the subject. He needed to know what—and who—he was dealing with.

He popped downstairs, tousled Will's hair, asked him how football practice was. To Nick's great relief, Will started talking and the kids took turns telling stories about their days throughout the entire meal. Occasionally, Nick would glance across the table at Beth and smile or wink after one of the kids said something funny or awkward, just as he always did, to demonstrate nothing had changed. For Beth's part, she seemed no different than the day before, or the day before that, although her mood in general since their return from Michigan had tilted toward chaotic anyway. It wasn't until the kids departed to the family room that she approached Nick, rubbed his shoulders, and asked if he was doing okay. The touch of her hands, normally inviting, left him cold.

"Doing good. I'm just tired. I had a long day. You?"

Her eyelids fluttered. She gave a little head tilt. "The same."

"Actually, I thought I'd retire early. If you're good with that, the kids?"

A hesitancy and a stare. "Of course. Get some sleep. You need it."

Yes, he certainly did. Although he was pretty sure sleep would come no easier tonight than it had any of the other nights over the past several days. He went upstairs and showered, pretended to conk out for the rest of the night.

Early the next morning, Jake slid from the bed, and the house, before Beth awoke. As soon as he arrived in his office in Cincinnati, he asked his assistant to reschedule a couple of meetings, then shut the door and texted Beth's parents in Florida. Expressing urgency, he told them he needed to speak with them as soon as possible and in private. The minute Beth's mother responded, Nick set up a video call.

They appeared on the screen huddled in their Florida kitchen, palm tree hand towels hanging from oak cabinets in the background. "Liz and John, sorry for the urgency, but I'm really in need of some information...and advice," Nick said.

Liz immediately panicked, as mothers were prone to do, and asked if Beth and the kids were okay. Her small, frail hands pulled at the collar of her shirt, crumpling the material in her fist.

"Yes, yes, everyone is fine," Nick said. He scratched his chin, wondering how to best approach the subject. He needed to know about the night in question but wanted to keep Missy Ferguson—and the discovery of her body—out of the conversation at all costs. Since Beth's parents lived in Florida now, they probably hadn't heard the news, and he preferred to keep it that way.

"I don't know if you're aware," Nick said, "but last week, Beth and I went to our twentieth high school reunion."

Liz nodded. "Yes, Beth said you were planning to attend."

"Has it been that long already?" John asked. He shook his head. "Doesn't seem possible." A quiet, studious man and small in stature, Nick had always liked Beth's father. He'd adopted her and treated her like his own when he didn't have to, and Nick admired him for doing so. "Did it go okay?"

"Well, not exactly," Nick said. "Beth had a little incident, out on the lake." He raised a palm toward the camera. "Again, she's fine, but..." He wrung his hands, cracked his knuckles. "Do you remember how Beth went into that...state after homecoming one year in high school? Like for a month, she was depressed and hard to reach? You took her to a doctor who diagnosed her with PTSD."

Liz made a little face, brushed back her dyed blond bob. She clutched more fabric. "Yes, of course," she said. "It was a terrible time. Beth...I'm not sure she even remembers most of it. She certainly doesn't like to talk about it."

"Yes, I know," Nick said. "She doesn't know that I'm aware of her treatment by a psychiatrist, and believe me, I don't intend to tell her otherwise, but I heard something at the reunion, and I'm wondering if other things also occurred during that time...things maybe I don't know about?"

Liz and John shared a glance. Her lips tightened into a razor-thin line.

"Somebody asked me about the time a park ranger found Beth out at the lake. They said that she drove, sleep-walked or something, to the lake and took a boat out?" He glanced at his office door over his shoulder, felt like he was exposing secrets he shouldn't. "They, uh, seemed pretty certain about it, and I was shocked. I told him I'd never heard of any such incident, and I just...I need to know what happened. Your version of events."

John said something indistinguishable to his wife, then spoke for them both. "Yes, it's true, Nick. Beth had an episode—I don't know if I would call it sleepwalking or, well, no one really knows—but she ended up out at the lake in a boat and a ranger later found her. The doctor said she might have gone out there to find peace—you know the lake was a happy place for her—but in her mental state and with the weather turning bad that night, she got lost."

"Her mental state, yes," Nick said, thinking about the timing of the incident. "I looked at the date this happened, and I was surprised to see that, although it was after homecoming, it occurred right around the beginning of her deep slide into depression. From what I remember, at least, Beth's dark time came after this incident. Would you agree?"

Liz seemed to think it over. "Yes, that's true. I would say she was upset and crying many days before, but this was the first truly alarming incident."

"I think, after homecoming, things built up in her mind," John said. "Then this happened, and all of that combined sent her to that dark place."

Yes, maybe. Or maybe something far darker occurred that none of them knew about. What would her parents think if they knew what Nick did right now? That their daughter's missing time in the marsh was the same night Nick had discovered Missy Ferguson dead on a lakeshore near the cabin?

"When you came to me, to ask me what happened to make her so depressed," Nick asked, "it was after this incident, right?"

They both nodded. "I'm sorry we didn't tell you, Nick," Liz said. "It was just, you were young and we knew how much you cared for Beth. After you told us about the allegations made against you and Beth's fight with that girl, we didn't feel it necessary to stress or traumatize you more than you already were at that point. And Beth, like I said, I don't think she even remembers now, and even if she did, I'm sure she would be too embarrassed to tell you."

A co-worker popped his head in Nick's office. Nick asked him to give him five.

"But what happened at the lake?" John asked. "You said there was an accident?"

"Yes. Beth took a boat out, rowed past the break into the path of an eight-man scull. There was a collision. She took a nasty hit to the head but she's fine. She seemed to not know why she rowed out that far. But this incident in her past may explain it. Rowing out to the lake may have triggered something, a memory of some kind."

The fine lines around Liz's eyes deepened. "The doctor said Beth may have repressed some memories of things that troubled her at that time. I know the events that occurred between her and that girl don't seem that drastic to you or I, or most of us, but Beth...you know how sensitive she can be."

Nick did. At least, he thought he did. Now, he wasn't so sure.

Not wanting to trouble her parents any further, he thanked them and hung up. Then he called the best psychiatrist he could find and made an appointment to talk later that afternoon. Dr. Felding, PhD, would be glad to speak with him on the topic of repressed memory.

Nick climbed the steps of the historic brick building with white trim and a little iron plaque outside listing Felding's name. His lobby was one of calm and nurturance, painted a light shade of green with a waterfall and an abundance of plants. The doctor, a reposed man of about forty with rectangular eyeglasses and a beard, greeted Nick then took him into another relaxed room with plenty of windows and a view of a park.

The doctor made himself comfortable in a studded brown leather chair with a tall back. "What can I help you with, Mr. Storvik? You mentioned something on the phone about a family member possibly dealing with some repressed memories?"

Without giving too much detail, Nick explained how a recent gathering had taken his family member to a place with many memories, most of them happy, but one somewhat tragic. "She got upset and left the group, then appeared to kind of black out for a time. Not physically, but mentally. Her doctor from the past said she possibly had repressed memories. What are those, exactly?"

"In general, a person represses the memory of an event when they find it particularly tragic or harmful. Whether physical or emotional pain, it must be of a severity to cause the brain to go into a sort of hibernation. If the brain believes the body and nervous system is at risk, it will shut down everything nonessential to protect itself. In this way, it's a bit like an alcoholic during a blackout. The memories might be there, but because the alcohol in the body is at such a level as to possibly injure, the brain shuts down nonessential functions."

Nick chewed at the skin around what used to be his nails, having already bit them down to the quick in the past week. "What kind of trauma would cause such a thing to happen? You said severe. How severe?"

"The most frequent cause of repressed memory I see is from some type of sexual abuse: rape, molestation, or incest. Other times it's a terrible accident, the death of a person close to them in a drowning or car accident, for example."

"In this case, what's most troubling to us is, that what happened to this family member to cause this reaction—as far as we know—wasn't anything too traumatic. Nothing like rape or sexual abuse, or even a terrible accident. That's what we can't understand," Nick said. "Repressing the memory seems like a bit of an overreaction."

Dr. Felding raised a bushy eyebrow. "Well, my initial inclination would be to say that there is likely more to the story or inciting event that anyone knows about. Every person is different in how they react to stress, but generally, if an act or incident caused this individual to repress the memory of it, it had to be something that tremendously shocked the system."

Nick glanced out the windows, eyed the setting sun, felt an immense grief and fear for his wife wash over him. What had Beth seen or done that rainy night out in the marsh? He had to find out, get it out in the open, for both their sakes. "Doctor? What would it take to surface memories such as these? Is there a technique or program you use to help someone remember?"

"Well, hypnosis often has the best success, performed after an extended period of counseling first, of course. As a doctor, I can tell you it's quite dangerous—to both the one conducting the hypnosis and the patient—to put a patient under hypnosis before having a good understanding and insight as to the type of individual they are and the likely occurrence that caused their repressed memory in the first place."

Hypnosis, of course. But totally out of the question. There was no way Nick could chance any third party performing such an act on Beth, unknowing as to whether she might confess to some unpardonable sin during such a session.

"Anything else?" Nick asked. "What about taking that individual back to the place it happened? Make the sights, sounds, and the mood the same as the night of the incident? Would doing something like that help?"

"Yes, oftentimes it does, but there is no guarantee. But you should know, it can make the victim erratic, even violent, if forced to try to recall something they have repressed."

Nick let out a deep breath, then stood and thanked the doctor for his time. He was pretty sure what he was going to have to do now, and Beth wasn't going to like it.

19

Confrontation

For the next five days, Nick and Beth circled around each other like rabid dogs, first one biting, then the other. The stress and pressure of the last two weeks had taken a toll. Nick no longer sensed that Beth trusted him, and he was no longer sure he trusted her. Every day, Beth alternated between bouts of rage or withdrawal and complained of intense migraines. The kids repeatedly asked what was wrong with her, only for Beth to snap at them and tell them to stop asking. Anna even broken into tears. He thought of attempting to tell her about Jake's visit and the positive news that he wasn't the father, only to realize admitting his relief would inform her of the obvious—that he had slept with Missy and Jake had taken his DNA without permission—neither of which he had confessed yet, and Nick worried what it would do to her. Beth was deteriorating quickly, the memories already surfacing fast and furious now.

By Friday morning, Nick had arranged for the kids to stay elsewhere for the weekend, and he was determined for him and Beth to get at the truth. He already had the car packed and ready to go.

No more lies. No more secrets. Not from either of them.

"Where are the kids?" Beth asked for the umpteenth time since arriving home.

"I told you. I gave them permission to stay with friends for the weekend."

"Anna is too young to stay anywhere, Nick." She threw her purse over her shoulder, grabbed her car keys. "Where the hell is she? I'm going to get her."

He stepped in front of his wife and gently took hold of Beth's shoulders. "She's fine, and no, you're not going to get her. We're going away for the weekend, to talk, to reconnect."

She pulled the cardigan she wore tighter around herself, like a straightjacket. "I'm not going anywhere. We just got home. I have a migraine and—"

"I know you do. That's why we're going away." He poured her a glass of wine. "Here. Relax."

She glanced at it, frowned. "No. The alcohol will just make it worse."

Nick sighed. This wasn't going to be easy. His plan was to give her a mild sedative with a glass of wine, let her sleep as he drove. If she were awake, she'd never let him drive where they needed to go. "How about tea then?" He filled the kettle, put it on the stove.

Behind him, he could sense his wife's fury. "Where are my children?"

"I told you they're fine."

Nick turned to see Beth's chest rising and falling with angry breaths. They exchanged glares that required no words—*I'm not going. Yes, you are.* The silence between them brewed for a few minutes before the tea kettle whistled. Beth narrowed her eyes, made a break for the stairs. "I'm calling the police."

Nick instinctively reached for her, ripped the phone from her hand. "You're doing no such thing."

And that was it. His once good plan descended into chaos. They ended up in their first physical match—Nick wrestling his wife into submission, bruising her arms, his wife scratching and slapping at his face. Neither was themselves now. They both thought they were fighting for their lives, no longer certain of the capabilities of the person they were married to. Nick was alarmed by Beth's physical violence, but the thing that bothered him even more was the utter fear his wife displayed of him, screaming and kicking at him as if he were about to murder her.

He told her repeatedly to calm down, but it was too late. Beth was burrowing into madness.

What could he do? There was no stopping this now. He couldn't call the police without him going to jail, without their marriage receiving a permanent scar. Nor could he release her only to see her continue to suffer and not face their truths. So, with great reluctance, Nick dragged his wife into the garage, secured her hands and feet with duct tape, and placed her in the backseat of his car. The next thing he knew, he was backing out onto the street and headed to the interstate.

Beth groaned and moaned from the back seat, crying one minute, then bursting into anger the next. She kicked at the door. At the back of his seat. "Stop the car, Nick," she shouted. "I mean it. Now!"

In the rearview mirror, he could see her wriggling and rolling across the seat, trying desperately to pull at the tape on her hands. He glanced down at the speedometer, realized he was doing eighty on the freeway. He could only imagine what would happen to him if an officer pulled him over and saw a woman, his wife, bound in the back seat.

He slowed the car to sixty-five. Tried to take several deep breaths, pull himself together.

But it was difficult. For three hours, it went like this, Beth fighting and begging, telling him he didn't have to do this. Nick driving, at times near tears, fearing for his wife. Near ten p.m., he pulled off the freeway and began to cruise the backroads, around curves and over hills that were all too familiar. The deeper into the country they drove, the darker it became, until the only light was a sliver of moon. He could sense Beth's mood change the minute the earthy smells of the lake became apparent, the various pondweed, duckweed, and bulrush permeating the air through the cracked-open window. Twenty minutes later, he stopped and got out amid the sounds of bullfrogs and crickets.

Again, she kicked at him with both feet as he attempted to pull her from the car. He prayed no one was nearby who could see him scoop her up from the back seat and close the car door. God only knew what they would imagine. She gasped upon seeing they were at the trailhead that led to several cabins near the lakeshore in their hometown. But not just any cabins—*the* cabin—where it had all begun.

"Here? You're taking me here?" she shouted.

Nick carried her down the trail. "What's wrong with here?"

"You know damn well what's wrong...I'm not going in there." She wriggled and squirmed in his arms, ramming him with tied fists. "I'm going to scream."

He dropped her to her feet, clasped a hand over her mouth, lowered his face to meet her eyes, now wide with fear. "The hell you are. What you're going to do, once and for all, is tell me everything you know about me and Missy Ferguson. You're finally going to confess the truth."

With his pocketknife, he cut the tape from her feet, commanded her to enter the cabin. Though she resisted, she was no match for her husband, six inches taller and one hundred pounds heavier than her.

He flipped on the light, sat her down at a small table. She glared at the bed, at him, with a hatred he'd never seen before. Just the glower alone told him something he never suspected—Beth knew all about this cabin, and what had occurred on that bed.

He closed the door and locked it, walked around the cabin to open the windows.

"What the hell are you doing?" she asked. Her face and cheeks were swollen from tears.

He turned from the window on the north side, pointed. "Was this the one?" he asked.

Beth fumed, turned away.

"Was this the one?" he asked again, just short of yelling.

She didn't answer, but she didn't need to. He could read the answer on her face. He cranked the window open then drew together the soft curtains, letting them billow inward by the breeze. Turned off all the lights and lit a candle on the nightstand just to the side of the bed. When he'd set up the place just as he remembered it from that night so long ago, he took a chair and placed it directly in front of Beth, then sat to face her.

"Tell me," he said. "All of it."

"Why are you doing this, Nick? Why?" She sniffled, trembling, wiped her eyes with her bound wrists. "Why did you bring me to this place? I don't want to be here."

"Beth, look at me," he said, resting a hand on each of her knees, and speaking gently now. "I know you don't want to be here. I don't either. But this has gone on long enough. We're going to talk about it tonight, all of it. We're going to put all our secrets on the table. You...and me."

"No, Nick. I don't want to. Why are you forcing me to do this? Why do you have me tied-up? So, after I tell you whatever you want to know, you can murder me, the way you did her? So, you can take me out to the preserve and bury me too? You'll never get away with this—never."

He bit down hard on his bottom lip, closed his eyes, felt them swell with tears. Did his wife really believe he'd killed Missy Ferguson and was now about to do the same to her? How in the hell did they get here?

He took several deep breaths, preparing himself for what was to come. Since his meeting with Dr. Felding the prior week, he'd repeatedly rehearsed the words he was about to say to his wife, practiced keeping calm and neutral regardless of how she came at him.

"Beth, I'm not here to hurt you. I'm here to help you. I promise not to harm you, but, before we begin, I need your assurance you won't harm me either. If I remove the tape, can I trust you to stop being violent with me?"

Her brow flinched. Only then did she suddenly seem to see the cuts and bruises on his face caused by her own hands. She glanced at her bound hands, nodded. After he cut the duct tape away, Beth absently rubbed at her wrists.

Nick tossed aside the tape, retrieved a couple of bottled waters for them. While he was away, he saw Beth glance at the door. "Can I ask you a question?" he said, returning to his seat. "Do you really believe I killed Missy Ferguson?"

She glanced across the room, toward the window and the bed, the hate and jealousy crawling through her veins like dozens of tiny spiders in pipes. "I saw you, Nick. I watched you right there," she said, pointing. "I came back from camp early to surprise you, and instead, I'm the one who got the shock of my life. Despite all your promises to wait for me, I watched you make love to Missy Ferguson. You know what that did to me?"

Beth's former tremble turned into a visible shake.

Nick lowered his head and sighed, feeling an immense sense of guilt and embarrassment overcome him. She'd watched? Had stood at the window and never said a word? He couldn't image what she must've thought of him.

He rubbed his face and the back of his neck. "Why didn't you tell me? All these years? Why did you make me lie to you?"

"I wanted you to confess."

He glanced up. "How could I? After the way you broke down later?"

Her cheeks flushed. It was Beth's turn to look embarrassed.

"Did you know she was pregnant?" Nick asked. "I mean, before homecoming?"

Beth nodded. "At the clinic, where I used to get my birth control pills. I was waiting for my appointment when Missy came charging out of one of the rooms. She was crying, tears running down her face, her hair a mess. This woman doctor came racing after her telling her not to do anything drastic.

"And when Missy saw me, she just stopped cold. All that mascara smudged across her cheeks. Snot running out of her nose. She just stood there staring at me with her hand over her stomach as if trying to protect her precious unborn child from me. And I knew. In that instant, I knew. She was pregnant and the baby was yours."

Her words were vicious, spittle running from the corner of her mouth. She stared up accusingly, her gaze sharp, pained. All this time, she'd kept this knowledge inside.

Nick wondered why she'd ever stayed with him.

He folded over, as if he might be sick. So many lies. His, hers.

"Now you answer," she demanded. "Did you know? Did she tell you she was pregnant?"

"Yes, and...no," he said, remaining curled into himself, unable to look at Beth's pained face. "She showed me the pregnancy test, but I had no way of knowing if it was mine. I made a mistake not confronting it, and her, head-on. I just wanted it to go away, not admit what I'd done. That's what made her so angry. Me ignoring her."

Beth began to cry fresh tears. The shaking increased, her breaths growing shallow. "So, you killed her?" Beth whispered. "Did you?"

His head shot up. "No. No, Beth, I didn't."

Her brow furrowed, unconvinced. She shook her head slowly, as if she were still in denial. Her teeth chattered now, like she was freezing. "You were here. I have visions of you..." Her gaze darted left and right; she appeared afraid to say it. "Nick, I have visions of you carrying her body."

Nick sat back, sensed the blood draining from his face. "What? Beth, that isn't possible. It's something you dreamed."

But was it? Or was it true?

"I thought so, but no. The first time I saw the vision was on the boat that day at our reunion, right before I ended up in the water. I willed it away, but ever since that day, it's kept coming back—in the shower, in the bath. In the rain the other day, I remembered even more. I was out in the marsh. I was out..." She clasped her head. "It hurts so bad. My head."

He left the chair and knelt before her. "Beth, honey, it's okay. I know you were in the marsh that night. I read the police report. They said you blacked out, that you couldn't answer their questions. So, what you need to tell me is, what do you remember about being out there that night? And why? Why were you there?"

Her face twisted and contorted into a variety of expressions, growing angry, suspicious. "I didn't say I was there. I said I saw you there. You, not me. Don't twist my words. You're trying to twist my words."

Seeing the defensiveness surface, he made an extra effort to keep calm and explain. He knew the memories were fighting for her attention now, trying to keep hidden and make themselves known at the same time.

"Beth, if you saw me, it had to be here, right here at the cabin that night. Do you remember that night? The evening of October 26, 1996? You know you were here, because you said it yourself, you saw me. And I was here, but not in the marsh. I came here to meet Missy, to talk about the baby, to make things right. But, I never had a chance, because when I arrived? She was already dead."

Beth shook her head violently. Held her hands over her ears. "No, no, no."

"Yes, Beth, yes," he said, more firmly now, removing her hands. "When I arrived here, Missy was already dead. I didn't kill her. I came out here to talk with her. Her parents had kicked her out. I felt responsible. I had an obligation to help her, but I never got that chance."

Her breaths intensified.

His own heart raced like the fastest car. "Did you know I was coming here, Beth? Did you follow me?"

A deep and decisive groan emitted from deep within his wife's lungs. It didn't sound human.

"Do you remember what happened when you arrived here? Did you encounter Missy? Did the two of you fight?" Then, delicately: "Whatever happened, Beth, I know you didn't mean to do it, and it's okay to tell me. I'm your husband. I'm going to protect you."

But Beth no longer appeared to be present. After her eyes briefly rolled to the back of her head, a person Nick didn't recognize emerged. She stood and slapped him with a force he didn't know she was capable of, then lashed out angrily. "You liar! You lie! Why are you trying to blame me when you know it was you? I didn't kill Missy Ferguson. I didn't kill Missy Ferguson!"

And then, she grabbed Nick's pocketknife from the table and lunged.

20

She's Come Undone

B eth's husband was trying to kill her. She was sure of it now, as certain as she was that Nick had murdered Missy Ferguson. Why else would she have memories of him carrying a body up an embankment through brush, grasses, and cattail as tall as his waist? Why else would he be holding secret conversations with attorneys and psychiatrists, even Jake Waters? Why else had he felt the need to bind her hands and feet and bring her here, of all places? It could only mean one thing—he knew the memories were resurfacing and it wouldn't be long until she uncovered the truth. So, now he was planning to get rid of the one and only witness to his crime—Beth.

It all made sense now—why it was so painful remembering that time. Why she'd blocked it out for so long. Nick had killed Missy and Beth had seen the whole thing. Now, Nick was on a mission to kill his wife in the same manner that he'd murdered his one-time tryst so many years ago. Kill and bury Beth and hope for another twenty years before the authorities discovered her. Or maybe he would stage her death to look like a suicide, guilt over killing Missy Ferguson herself. She didn't put it past him. Already, he was trying to lay the blame on her.

Afterward, poor shell-shocked Nick would have to carry on without her and start anew. He would hold press conferences, cry false tears, hug his—their—children with false grief.

Such audacity. Such nerve.

She lunged toward him a second time, but he jumped back and she missed. The first time, she'd connected nicely with his hand as he'd raised it in self-defense, and the one-inch slice was bleeding now, and the blood was running down his arm and dripping on the floor. Nick genuinely appeared frightened of her, circling around the room, his hands up by his sides, but she knew—she was the one who had everything to fear.

"Beth?" he said. "What the hell is wrong with you? Put the knife down."

"No. No, I don't trust you anymore. I don't know who you are." She pushed the knife out farther in front of her, made wide-sweeping motions. "You're lying to me. Trying to make me sound crazy. Asking me to remember, then trying to convince me that I had something to do with Missy's death. You lie! You've always been lying!"

More circling, Nick keeping obstacles between them. "Who has always been there for you, Beth? Protected you? Saved you? I'm your husband. You do know me. I have no reason to harm you now." His voice was strangely calm, placating.

"Yes, you do, because you don't want to take responsibility for what you did. And you're trying to blame me. Why? Why, Nick?" A dark veil of betrayal overwhelmed her, and she began to cry again, at first a whimper, then harder, until the sobs hurt her chest. The knife trembled wildly before her and she had to grab it with both hands to try and steady it. Between the blur of tears that fell down her cheeks like heavy rain on the windshield, she could see Nick fade into nothing more than a distant image, as if he were moving away from her.

He was. He fled from the door and into the dark. Beth followed.

Outside, the wind whistled and blew, autumn leaves scattering from their branches as if they were fleeing the scene of a crime. Nick ran down the trail, but he was too tall to disappear, the grasses barely thigh level. Beth pursued him, but she didn't understand why. She knew she should turn back, get the car keys, go to the police—yet, she didn't. She just kept on running down that trail, the same one she'd fled so many years ago after seeing Nick and Missy in the cabin. Down, until she reached the lakefront, where Nick stood near a row-boat.

Beth gasped at the sight of the boat, at Nick standing there in silhouette.

The pain in her head burst like the pop of a balloon, followed by a jarring flash of light and energy. Images streamed into her consciousness, one after another. Visions of an approaching storm off to the east, with a dark wall of clouds only visible in the lightning. A field of nannyberry, spicebush, and willows off to the right swaying like animal tails in the increasing wind. Missy Ferguson standing on the bank of the lake, her hair blowing across her face, eyes squinting at the figure approaching her. Then closer, her face, her hollowed cheekbones, her thin lips, expressing her displeasure at the sight before her. A figure too small, a shadow too narrow. Not the person Missy expected. Not Nick Storvik at all. But his girlfriend, Beth McCallum.

Beth's body shook as she sensed the blind rage that had overtaken her at that moment so many years ago. It infested itself in her blood and bones like a treacherous cancer that couldn't or wouldn't become contained. No amount of reason, no explanation, no argument could possibly change the wrath she was about to unleash.

First were the traded barbs and insults between Missy and her, the threats of harm if Missy didn't leave Nick alone and Beth didn't leave, period. This, followed by Beth moving forward and shoving Missy backward, only for Missy to respond with a strike to Beth's face. Then came the fight—both hitting, slapping, and clawing at each other until the two of them went down in a twisting, turning mass of bodies. It was then the skies opened with a fury that only matched Beth's anger, causing the sandy ground to loosen and for them to slip and fall and slide ever closer to the lakeshore.

The last time Beth stumbled, she found herself face-down with Missy on top of her, pushing her head farther into the rocky, wet sand. And as the water pooled from the lake, a mix of sand and water quickly filled her nose and mouth, and Beth had the sense that she was going to drown. She began to buck and kick like a horse until she felt the weight above her release.

She gasped for air, clinging to life.

But Missy was coming back for another round.

Charging forward with all her fury, Beth tackled Missy head-on in the stomach and landed her flat on her back. Now it was Beth on top of her, at first pounding, then grabbing both sides of Missy's head and bashing it upon the ground. Except beneath Missy's head hadn't been the grindy, rocky sand that made up the beach here, but a jagged piece of stone, rugged and uneven, and the second time Beth pounded Missy's head back upon it, blood pooled from underneath, covering the area with a thick, dark substance. Missy's arms stopped flailing and she reached for her head, her breaths sounding harsh and thick.

Realizing she'd hurt Missy, Beth stood and wiped the blood from her mouth where Missy had hit her, then turned and went back to the boat. She would leave. The head wound would be enough. It would teach her a lesson. But no, somehow Missy got up and started to stagger toward Beth, calling her a bitch while holding the back of her bleeding head. Then she started to taunt Beth, telling her how good Nick had felt and tasted, and Beth had heard enough. Missy just couldn't leave well enough alone. So, Beth grabbed the oar from the boat and swung it like a baseball bat, landing the blade straight to the side of Missy's head.

And this time Missy went down, and she didn't get up.

Beth froze there in the wind, as paralyzed and unflinching as she now stood, getting soaked and waiting for Missy to come at her again. But nothing happened. For a minute, then five, Missy lay crumpled motionless on the ground. Above, the lightning crackled and the thunder roared, and as the rain intensified, the same mix of sandy mud began to consume parts of Missy's face just as it had done Beth's minutes before. Beth, starting to feel a wave of panic and anxiety overtake her, moved closer. She needed to know if Missy was still alive, if she was breathing. Slowly, she inched forward and leaned over to remove the wet strands of hair that covered Missy's face.

And there it was, her eye, open and unflinching, just as in the Edgar Allan Poe story—the veiled pale evil eye.

Beth jumped back and fell. Suddenly, from up on the hill, a voice called out. Yelling for Missy. She couldn't distinguish it then, but now, she knew. That voice, it had been Nick. Nick arriving to meet Missy. But Missy couldn't respond because she was dead. Because Beth had killed her.

21

Memories

Nick Storvik watched as his wife dropped the pocketknife and fell to her knees. He quickly rushed to retrieve it, then fell to the ground beside her. She looked like a remnant of herself, a shell of the woman he'd known for twenty-four years. Her head lolled backward upon her shoulders and a cry emitted from deep within her throat, a wail like the guttural scream of a mother who'd just lost her child, or perhaps—a woman who'd just realized she'd taken the life of another many years ago. Nick was afraid to touch her, scared his fingers would feel like fire and brimstone upon her skin, given the state she was in, but carefully wrapped an arm beneath her waist and across her shoulders to cradle her in his arms. There was nobody he could call now, no doctor to help her. No, they were in this together, just as they were on that cold, dark night in the Michigan preserve so many years ago.

They just hadn't known it at the time.

"Beth? Can you hear me?" he asked.

Rigidity. More cries.

She jerked, convulsed, as if she were having a seizure. He took her back inside the cabin, grabbed pillows from the bed, placed them around her. Moved furniture out of the way. Re-cradled her.

Nick froze and listened, his every muscle rigid, before a scream the like of which he'd never heard shot from his wife's mouth. He prayed the cabins were empty enough that no one would hear. "She's not moving. Why? There's so much blood." More jerking. "Oh my God, I killed her. I killed her!"

His skin crawled with her confession.

She went limp.

"Beth, honey, can you hear me?" He shook her body. He didn't know if he should be talking to her, or just letting the memories play out. It was beyond frightening to see her like this, limp and unresponsive.

Beth's eyes flashed open. Blinked. Jerked. Blinked again.

"All my fault," she muttered.

But, it wasn't. Not solely anyway. Beth had played a role, but also Missy, and most certainly, Nick. His weakness to resist Missy and wait a month had caused this mess—and ultimately, Missy's belief that Nick had gotten her pregnant and Beth's response. It was as if the three of them had circled around each other and created a trifecta of perfectly bad actions and reactions resulting in betrayal, murder, and cover-up.

He wondered how it all could've conjoined to take such a horrible direction. Once again, he felt the weight of the responsibility and guilt consume him. What would Beth think when she discovered that it was Nick who'd arrived at the cabin to discover Missy dead and decided to bury her body instead of call in the local authorities? That, in fear for his own life, a life as a convicted murderer and years spent in prison, he'd risked moving Missy from the cabin to the trunk of his car, then driven out to the preserve to bury her?

Ironic to think now, he'd been protecting Beth too. He just hadn't known it at the time.

For the next several hours, Nick sat beside Beth and let her mind and memories play through the drama. He placed a brown paper bag over her nose and mouth and told her to breathe slowly as needed, continuing to keep his voice low and calm, and repeating that she was in a safe place. When she finally came to, he removed the bag, wrapped his arms around his wife, and held her while she cried it out.

I promise to love you with all my heart and soul, to be the love in lover, the care in caretaker, the provide in provider. I promise to create and support a family with you, in a household filled with laughter, patience, understanding, and love. I vow not just to grow old together, but to grow together. I love all that I know about you now, and I will love all there is to learn about you in the future. I promise to always be your biggest fan, as well as your partner in crime. I will love you faithfully, not just through the easy times, but through the most difficult of times. Whatever may come, I will always be there. As I have given you my hand, so I give you my life—to keep, to cherish, to protect. I would gladly give my life for you, and promise to protect, honor, and shelter you and our children forever. I trust you in all that you do now, and all that you decide for us in the future.

22

The Tell-Tale Heart

I t was a cool, crisp early-autumn day in September, five years later. The classmates attending the twenty-fifth reunion had gathered around a barbeque at the lake, grilling hamburgers and hot dogs and telling stories of their former glory days. It was the kind of day Midwesterners loved to enjoy outside, one Beth and Nick would normally spend watching a football game or working in the yard raking leaves and pruning the garden.

But today Beth had other plans.

Nick had asked her not to go, had in fact not wanted to attend the reunion at all, fearing a repeat of the one five years earlier, but Beth had insisted, wanting closure, and to prove to her classmates, especially Jake Waters, that she and Nick had nothing to hide. Over the years, Jake had tried, unsuccessfully, to convince the local district attorney that Beth could've murdered Missy Ferguson, but beyond her possible motive and some hearsay from classmates that the earring belonged to Beth, Jake couldn't prove that Missy Ferguson had died the same night the park ranger had discovered Beth in the marsh, nor explain how Beth could've possibly buried Missy's body.

He'd then tried to place blame on Nick and Beth, that they'd acted and killed Missy together, but nobody believed Nick would leave Beth out in the marsh alone to possibly die in the cold after they'd buried Missy's body together.

Jake had also investigated a classmate from Missy's former high school after discovering he was the true father of Missy's child, but that man had been attending college that autumn at an institution more than a thousand miles away when Missy disappeared. All in all, Jake Waters didn't have enough evidence to put all the pieces together to make a solid case.

After a quick kiss on the cheek and squeeze of his hand, Beth discreetly left the reunion, wanting to do this while the others were gathered. She needed to do this, to put this behind her—and them—once and for all.

Dressed in jeans, calf-high boots, and a shawl, she listened as her steps clamored along the solemn walkway through the shady graveyard high on a hill overlooking the town and the lake below. In her hands, she held two roses, one for Missy Ferguson and one for her unborn baby. One an offering from Beth and one from Nick.

Surrounding her were the ghosts of generations past, some as far back as the early nineteenth century. Most of the headstones were crumbling and difficult to read, but included many who'd died in the cholera epidemic of the 1820's and the clashes over land rights between the Iroquois and settlers later in the mid-century. As she approached the more recent gravestones, her anxiety began to make itself known— the clammy skin, the shortness of breath, the racing heartbeat.

Thump, thump, thump, thump.

She stopped momentarily to close her eyes and inhale the air and absorb the nature surrounding her. In the wind, she could hear the leaves whisper and flutter, the nearby grasses gently sway. The air held a slightly earthy smell, of dew-soaked brush and decaying leaves.

She opened her eyes to view the expanse of oaks and maples on the property and the adjoining vacant land to the north, awaiting future arrivals. She wondered how many of the people buried here had met an untimely death, had experienced their final breaths at the hands of someone they loved or were related to? Or worse, like Missy, a rival?

A crisp breeze scattered downed leaves, most of them felled by the prior week's heavy wind and rain instead of the fading light of autumn. She glanced up into the blue sky, feeling God observing as the leaves blew around her feet and swirled up in an unseen suction of air. After taking a deep breath, she continued walking down the path, past the headstone of a young woman with angels two feet tall protecting both sides, past a towering monument to a family patriarch and matriarch, past the tiniest headstone of a child just three years old. Who decided how much time we had on earth? Was it God and pre-destination? Or just random chance of body and disease? Beth didn't know anymore, but she couldn't imagine a God who'd planned for Missy to die at the hands of Beth's jealousy and rage, so she leaned on the side of chance.

Around a bend, at the edge of a ridge that overlooked the rolling hills of the adjacent county, including a small white church with a steeple, sat a gravestone with the name *Ferguson*. The date of death noted on the marker was twenty-seven years old but the stone itself appeared fairly new, and included an homage to an unborn baby, something that may have made those passing by pause and take notice.

They would wonder: Why did this stone appear so new when the death was more than two decades ago? Had the woman been missing or unidentified for some time?

What had taken so long for authorities to discover her and bring her to this place of peaceful rest?

The locals would know the reasons, but only Beth knew the answer.

The person you see now standing before her grave.

Trembling, Beth knelt in front of the stone, both knees resting on the grass that most certainly was directly above Missy's body, holding the roses in her hands. Closing her eyes, she whispered a short prayer for forgiveness and understanding, a plea for peace. She apologized for overreacting, for pushing Missy backward to stumble across that rock, but she couldn't help but admonish Missy for being so aggressive and pursuing Nick in the first place. She asked many a question why—why Missy couldn't have lusted after someone else, why she hadn't used birth control, why she couldn't have just taken care of matters on her own after the fact. She spoke of the grief that Missy's actions had caused many people, including Missy's parents, then, realizing her selfishness, backtracked, and again apologized for her role in the situation. Then she sat quietly and waited for an answer.

It wasn't what she wanted. As Beth sat there, the breeze blowing through her hair, she thought she could almost hear it, a low jarring *whump* that caused her to travel back in time to her English class, when her teacher read those words. Except they no longer seemed like words, but actual human heartbeats. Now, more than ever, she sensed the level of guilt that plagued her heart.

"It was a low, dull, quick sound—much a sound as a watch makes when enveloped in cotton. I gasped for breath— and yet the officers heard it not. I talked more quickly—more vehemently; but the noise steadily increased... It grew louder—louder—louder! And still the men chatted pleasantly and smiled. Was it possible they heard not? Almighty God—no, no! They heard, they suspected, they knew! They were making a mockery of my horror."

Beth quickly placed the roses, her hands trembling. She needed to make that sound stop. "I'm sorry, I'm sorry. I truly am," she said through hushed breath. "But you crossed a line. Nick Storvik was mine and always will be." She quickly stood, turned, and began to walk briskly back down the path.

Thump, thump, thump. Please stop the beating of that hideous heart.

Thump, thump, thump. A second small heartbeat responded.

"Louder—louder—louder!"

And suddenly, she could feel not one eye—that pale filmy blue death eye—staring back at her, but two, watching her from their combined grave with their insidious hearts still beating.

Thump, thump, thump.

Beth broke out in a near run, her boots clattering against the pavement all the way down the hill and through the older parts of the graveyard. For a moment, she worried that she would rouse them all—the ghosts—as if all those bodies lying in their death-beds would wake and rise. At the bottom of the hill, she clasped her hands over her ears until she could rid herself of the dreadful noise from high above. She gasped for breath, tried to shake off the cold chills that gripped the back of her neck. She made a break for the street and unlocked her car with the key fob, but as she approached, saw a figure standing there, arms crossed. Like always, he wore jeans, boots, and a sport coat.

"Beth," Jake said.

"Jake," Beth acknowledged between breaths. She started for the car door, but he refused to move out of the way.

"You okay? You seem a bit upset," he said. "Like you saw a ghost."

She shuddered, praying the hair on the back of her neck had returned to its proper place. "I'm fine." She'd hoped after all Jake's former inquisitions to not see his dark eyes anymore, but there they were, examining her with all their prior suspicions. He must've been lying in hiding at the reunion, waiting and wondering if she and Nick would make an appearance. She should've known as much, heeded Nick's warning not to come.

"Nice day for a visit. Anyone special?"

Beth shuffled her feet, turned in a circle. "I'm just paying respects—for the entire class."

He huffed. "Is that so? Why you?"

She met his eyes, saw the accusation, the knowledge of what she'd done. As the whispers of wind and rumor passed between them, she could still hear those heartbeats, theirs and hers, the tell-tale heart. *"Dissemble no more! I admit the deed!"*

But she wouldn't.

"Why not me, Jake?" She grabbed the door handle and slid into the car. Bid adieu to Jake Waters. She would never, ever crack and neither would Nick. Now that each knew the truth of what had happened in that marsh that night, how they'd cared for and protected each other just like their vows—even without knowing the other's deeds—they would take their knowledge to the grave.

Until death do us part.

ABOUT THE AUTHOR

Lori Lacefield is the author of suspense and thriller novels. Her first two suspense thrillers, **The Advocate** and **The Fifth Juror**, were released in May 2018. Both are part of the Women of Redemption series, featuring women who may not be perfect, but perfectly kick-ass when given a second chance.

Her first two thriller novels, **99 Truths** and **The Art of Obsession**, featuring FBI Agent Frankie Johnson, local profiler, will be released in the spring of 2019. You can read the first short story featuring Agent Frankie Johnson, **The Fire Keeper**, in **Burning: An Anthology of Short Thrillers** available on Amazon.com.

To learn more about Lori, enter her giveaways, sign up for future news and events, and get additional free content and bonus books, go to https://www.lorilacefield.com/

Made in the USA
San Bernardino,
CA